Courageous Heart

by

Christine Bush

Christine Bush

Formerly published as Warning at Eagle's Watch

Without limiting the rights under copyright reserved above, no part of this publication may be reproduced, stored in or introduced into a retrieval system, or transmitted, in any form, or by any means (electronic, mechanical, photocopying, recording, or otherwise) without the prior permission of the copyright owner.

Please Note

This is a work of fiction. Names, characters, places, and incidents either are the product of the author's imagination or are used fictitiously, and any resemblance to actual persons, living or dead, business establishments, events or locales is entirely coincidental.

The scanning, uploading, and distributing of this book via the internet or via any other means without the permission of the copyright owner is illegal and punishable by law. Please purchase only authorized electronic editions, and do not participate in or encourage electronic piracy of copyrighted materials. Your support of the author's rights is appreciated.

© Copyright 1979, 2011, 2013 by Christine Bush

Cover and eBook design by eBook Prep www.ebookprep.com **Thank You**.

3

To my wonderful children: David, Abby, Sue, Reeny and Jackie

Christine Bush

Chapter 1

Hillary downshifted her little green Volkswagen to relieve the noisy strain of the engine as the road ahead of her climbed steadily. As the gears meshed again, the engine sounded a little better, though the car remained reluctant to continue the long ascent. Like Hillary herself.

She sighed quietly and tossed her head, relaxing the tense muscles in the back of her neck. Her shoulder-length red hair bounced softly with the movement and then fell back into place.

Well, the trip would soon be over. She'd soon be there. She tried to ignore the little knot that was tightening in the pit of her stomach.

For hours she had driven the little green car up the jagged coastline of New England, following the route she had carefully marked on the road map that lay on the seat beside her. She was in Maine now, and soon she would be entering the town of Highpoint. Eagle's Watch was supposed to be just a few miles beyond.

Eagle's Watch. It was a place she had never even heard of until three short days ago. A place that would now be her home for an indefinite period of time.

She felt as if someone were holding a downy pillow over her freckled face smothering the life out of her. She felt trapped.

And how had this happened to Hillary Holt? What turn of events, what string of circumstances, had brought her here? It really boiled down to a very simple rule of thumb: Nothing in life is free!

When her parents had died, she had been an impressionable fourteen years of age, alone, and penniless. She held no grudge against her parents for the situation she found herself in. Indeed, they had worked all their lives to keep their heads above water, to keep their small and happy family together and healthy.

But it hadn't been easy. And when the fatal car wreck had claimed their lives, Hillary had been left with only her happy remembrances of their love and a large pile of overdue bills. She had been barely old enough to grasp the hopelessness of her unhappy situation.

But her luck had changed. The miracle came in the form of a letter, a letter from a prominent attorney in London to the kindly but frustrated family lawyer who was vainly trying to unravel the chaos that was the Holt family estate.

The London attorney had written, succinctly and formally, that a trust fund for the education of Hillary Holt, recently orphaned daughter of Henry and Mary Holt of Philadelphia, had been established by Miss Matilda Waverly, currently of London.

Miss Matilda, as Hillary soon found out, was a spinster aunt of her mother's. She was supposedly close to eighty, and had nothing to do with any of the family for a number of years. Yet somewhere in the back of her mind, she had a soft spot for her young niece Mary—Hillary's mother, whom she had met only once. There had been no offer of love or a home for the young girl who was Mary's only daughter, no personal contact with Hillary at all during the elaborate legal proceedings.

And yet, at fourteen, she had not questioned or even wondered about the actions. She had happily, and with untold relief, thanked God for the miracle that had given her some direction in her life.

She had been sent off to a private boarding school, followed by a few years of hard study and practice at a prestigious nursing school in Philadelphia. The bills had been wordlessly paid, and Hillary had put every ounce of concentration she could muster into her rigorous training. She had never heard from Miss Matilda again.

Until this week.

In the beginning, Hillary had been curious, grateful, eager to keep in contact with the unknown woman who reopened the doors in a life that she feared had been slammed shut forever. She inquired through her lawyer about an address so she could mail letters, send Christmas cards. But the lawyer quietly and efficiently tabled Hillary's questions and attempts to contact Miss Matilda, saying that the girl's would-be letters were unnecessary, and most probably unwanted.

And so gradually Hillary pushed Miss Matilda to the back of her mind, and had gone on with her life as best she could.

So far she had done well. Hillary's decision to become a nurse came soon after she had settled into her boarding school, and since that time, she had put much effort into the schoolwork that was the basis for her acceptance into the nursing school.

Each passing day in the classrooms and on the hospital wards greatly reinforced Hillary's wonder and her dedication to the medical profession that she had chosen.

Her training was well rounded and complete. She had worked amazingly hard, often denying herself the social pleasures and pastimes that many of her classmates enjoyed.

In her final year, she found the branch of nursing that she knew instinctively was right for her. Surgical nursing. At the first operation she witnessed, sitting high above the table in the glassed-in gallery of the operating room, she felt a feeling of wonderment come over her as she watched the surgeon's deft hands perform his life-saving task. And at his side, cleanly scrubbed and alert, stood his efficient and knowledgeable nurse.

Many of the other girls in the class felt squeamish and uncomfortable observing the procedure. Their nervous giggles and protests had echoed in the halls of the nurses' dormitory late into the night.

But Hillary had been strangely quiet and very sure. She found the type of work that she wanted to do. To see miracles performed daily right before her eyes, to assist in complicated procedures that could save limbs, organs, even life itself. It would be no easy task to be competent and disciplined enough to succeed, she knew. But she was determined to try.

And so she worked almost nonstop for the remainder of her time at nursing school, and had graduated with the highest honors.

Soon afterward, she was offered a position on the staff of her training hospital, working hand in hand with those same surgeons who had taught her so much. It was the chance of a lifetime. A chance to learn more and more, to grow constantly in her skills, a chance to realize her dream. She had been very happy.

Hillary was also very, very grateful to her unknown great-aunt, Miss Matilda, who had made it all possible for her.

And then the letter had arrived. It was written on several sheets of delicate rose-scented paper, in a thin, spidery hand. It had come from London, England.

My dear Hillary:

I was immensely delighted to hear of your successful completion of the nursing program. Such dedication and drive for personal achievement is so often lacking in the young today. It is because of this commendable trait that I am writing to you.

My request is a simple one, but nevertheless one which means a great deal to me. My oldest and dearest friend, Priscilla Scott, finds herself in need of expert nursing care. She has recently succumbed to a stroke which has unfortunately confined her to a wheelchair.

Her ancestral estate, Eagle's Watch, on the northern coastline of Maine, is quite remote and I gather there has been some difficulty in obtaining a suitable nurse/companion to ease her difficult days.

It would greatly delight me if you would consider accepting this position for my dear friend. If Eagle's Watch is even remotely as I remember it in my early years, you will find it a rare experience in solitude and tranquility.

Details, as always, will be handled through our competent attorneys.

Most gratefully,
Miss Matilda

That rose-scented letter changed Hillary's life. At first she had been tempted to rip it up deliberately, to refuse the request that her benefactress had made. But she could not.

For even as she was determined and dutiful in her work at the hospital, so was she conscientious and just in her personal life. She owed so much to the old woman who had written that letter, and she had never had to repay her benefactress.

Until now.

Legally, Hillary knew that she could walk away from the situation if she wanted to. But she felt a moral obligation to Miss Matilda. And that was that.

So Hillary had gone to her attorney and he laid out the details for her, giving her directions, telling her when she was to arrive at Eagle's Watch to assume her new role. The lawyer had shown no doubt, no surprise, that she would do Miss Matilda's bidding. Indeed, he assumed that she would take on the job.

And so here she was, in her battered old VW, covering the miles to Eagle's Watch and to the old woman for whom she was now responsible. Her career in surgery had been sidetracked temporarily, perhaps even permanently, with her refusal of the sought-after position on the surgery staff at the hospital. It was replaced by a job promising "solitude and tranquility." She turned her freckled nose up in disgust. The last thing she wanted was a quiet, remote life, cooped up with a demanding old woman who needed more mothering than nursing, in an isolated, empty house that must be quite unappealing, since no nurse would consent to live in it without coercion.

But Hillary brushed away the single tear that slid down her cheek, and she made an inner decision to make the best of her present circumstances, to do her best with a smile on her face, and to remain forever optimistic that the doors to her yearned-for future were not locked forever.

The tired little car quickly passed through Highpoint, a small little seacoast town, and she drove the steep, winding road upward, through the woods, for the last few miles.

And then she was there. Hillary could see no house from the narrow road, but two enormous stone pillars marked the drive, supporting a stately wrought-iron banner that said EAGLE'S WATCH.

She closed her tired eyes for a brief instant and muttered a little prayer. Then she drove very slowly down the gravel drive that led to Eagle's Watch. Pushing in on every side were dense clumps of pine and cedar trees, their massive branches interlocking to block out all but a very few of the late afternoon sun's rays.

The smell of evergreens filled Hillary's nostrils with their freshly clean aroma as she took the turns of the winding drive.

Suddenly the trees thinned out, giving her the feeling that she had emerged from a long tunnel. She made one more turn. Then she saw it—Eagle's Watch. Hillary's mouth was open in wonder, her green eyes wide, as she stopped the car.

The line of trees had stopped, leaving only a rocky surface for several hundred yards ahead. And sitting on the highest point of that huge, rocky expanse, silhouetted sharply against the summer blue sky, was the old structure. It was gray, a slightly lighter shade than the gray of the rocks that made up the landscape around it. And it was a castle.

Hillary, in truth, had never seen a castle in her life, but the edifice that loomed before her fit every fairy-tale description that she had ever heard. It was square and immensely solid looking, with two thick round turrets rising high from each end. There were many, many windows visible in the thick gray walls of the building, and a tremendous black door sat squarely in the middle.

"It's impossible," her brain screamed, "for something like this to exist!" She felt as if she had suddenly plunged backward in time, to the days of knights and dragons and damsels in distress. She hastily glanced at the base of the castle, and was somehow reassured to see that it was not surrounded by a moat.

She was to live *here*? It seemed incredible. It was incredible. How could anyone live in a place like this?

Hillary sat momentarily staring at the sight that greeted her eyes. There wasn't a single sign of life. She closed her eyes and listened. A steady rumble, a rhythmic roar reached her ears. The ocean was nearby.

She followed the remainder of the drive, which wound through the rocks and curved toward the left side of the castle. She slowed to a stop. Her heart was pounding as she shut off the engine and climbed out of her confining seat. Just what was she getting herself into?

Drawn by the sound of the waves, and still hesitant to approach the menacing black door that loomed so ominously at the front of the castle, she skirted the building carefully, staying on the gravel path that led toward the ocean.

As she cleared the left side of the house, a magnificent sight stood before her. The castle stood on the very brink of a cliff, high and jagged. She stood on the edge and looked down. The white foamy waves of the Atlantic beat mercilessly on the rocks below.

The sun was bright and cast its summer beams on the nearby rocks, making them sparkle, making the surf look spectacular in its tints of blue and green. In front of her stretched the great expanse of ocean, with no land to be seen, except for a tiny spit of green that protruded down the rocky coast, supporting a tall lighthouse at its point.

It was a beautiful sight. But it was a lonely sight. How would she, a girl born and bred in the bustle of the city, survive in such a place? Eagle's Watch, it was called. But no eagles could be seen. She turned abruptly and walked back to face her employer.

Hillary rapped loudly on the heavy door with the massive brass knocker that adorned it, and stood back quietly, almost hoping that her knock would go unanswered. But that was not to be. The huge door opened noiselessly before her.

She felt a rush of cold air as the heavy door was pulled back. A small, middle-aged woman peered out at her, her graying hair pulled back from her face. A starched white cap sat on her head, and her slight body was clothed in a severe black uniform and crisp white apron.

"Come in, Nurse Holt. You are expected." She had spoken before Hillary had had a chance to open her mouth, the words rasping out in a dry, brittle voice. Then she stepped backward and motioned for Hillary to enter the door.

"Thank you," Hillary stammered, ill at ease and self-conscious before the frank stare that the little woman made no effort to hide.

"I am Mrs. Raymond, Miss Scott's housekeeper. I will show you to your room now, and my husband will fetch your luggage from the car. Miss Scott will wish to see you directly, I am sure. Follow me please."

The little housekeeper wasted no words on amenities. She was brusque and without the slightest trace of warmth. Hillary had no choice but to follow her uniformed back. They crossed the large stone foyer and headed for the wide stairway that rose before them. Hillary glanced with avid curiosity at massive stone walls, at the distant ceilings that seemed to mock her presence.

It was dim here, the illumination in the foyer coming from a few small electric lights, designed to look like candle sconces, stationed along the walls. They cast a shadowy glow, and Hillary suppressed a little shiver as her footsteps echoed smartly on the stone floor.

Up the stairs they traveled, past long rows of painted portraits of the former residents of Eagle's Watch, standing stiff and erect in their dated finery. They made an intriguing sight, and one which Hillary would have loved to study, but the efficient Mrs. Raymond bustled her along. Toward the top of the flight, the stairway made a sharp turn to the right, past an open balcony that offered a good view of the large foyer below.

Moving through a tall archway, they came upon a long, gracious corridor. The housekeeper opened the first door on the right.

"This will be your room, Nurse Holt. Miss Scott's suite is right next door. I am sure you'd like to freshen up after your long journey, and to change into something more appropriate." Her nose had a peculiar pinched look about it as she gazed disapprovingly at the pale yellow pantsuit Hillary had worn for the trip.

"I'll return in twenty minutes to bring you to Miss Scott."

She was gone. Hillary stood dumbfounded at the door to her room, feeling a mixture of annoyance at the woman who had regarded her with such obvious distaste and mirth at the ridiculousness of the entire situation. Was this for real? The mirth finally won out, and a little giggle began to rise in her throat as she ducked into her room.

Hillary looked around her and saw the room for the first time. A surge of delight ran through her. It was spacious and airy, amazingly bright compared to the small bit of the dark castle that she had seen so far. The carpet, drapes, and walls were decorated tastefully in soft shades of green. Three square windows occupied the far wall, standing open now. A slight breeze drifted in, rustling the soft curtains.

The furniture was attractive and modern, her small bathroom sparkling and very adequate. It was a room that she knew she could be very comfortable in, an oasis away from the dreariness of the castle below.

A sullen, quiet man knocked at the door and entered with her luggage, a few simple suitcases containing all of her worldly possessions. He was dressed in rough work clothes, showing signs of recent outdoor work on the huge estate. She thanked him briefly, and he was gone, being even less talkative than his bristly wife.

Hillary turned to her bags, ever mindful of the minutes rapidly slipping away. Mrs. Raymond would be at her door once again in a very short time, and she felt compelled to be ready and waiting.

She giggled at the thought of the dour housekeeper. Such strange inhabitants of Eagle's Watch she had met so far! Were they any indication of the personality of the mistress whom she had yet to meet? Would she be able to get along with Priscilla Scott?

She was determined to make a go of things. Someday, she thought with a grin, she might even look back at it all and have a good laugh. After all, how many people could say that they had resided in the dark depths of a medieval castle?

Opening one suitcase and extracting a freshly laundered uniform, white and trim, Hillary said a silent prayer of thanks for permanent press. She washed quickly in the little bathroom and changed her clothes. White dress, white stockings and shoes, white cap. She looked into the full mirror on the bathroom door, regarding the girl who gazed back at her. She studied the red hair, which hung gracefully to her shoulders, turning under slightly at the ends. Her thick bangs barely touched her eyebrows, bringing out the softness in her large, green eyes.

She wrinkled her nose as she looked at it, pert and turned up. It gave an inkling that its strong-minded owner was easy to laugh, as well as easy to get angry. Her mouth was red, and a bit too large, and her freckles stood out sharply against her pale skin.

Not a pretty face, she told herself. Just a face. But it was a face that came to life with her sparkling green eyes and her smiling mouth. She smoothed the nurse's uniform over her trim figure and gave a last sigh. She was ready for "smiley" Mrs. Raymond.

Chapter 2

A few moments later, after surviving the critical glance that showed a trace of approval for her neat and professional look, Hillary accompanied Mrs. Raymond down the corridor to the next door.

"She's waiting for you, Nurse Holt." The housekeeper paused as if groping for the right words. "You may find her a little—well, a little temperamental." She fidgeted a bit, then added, "I'll leave you now. You can ring for me when you need me."

She scurried off almost as if she couldn't get away from the closed bedroom door soon enough. Was she afraid of her employer? And if so, just what was Hillary getting herself into?

Well, she'd soon find out. She had come this far, and she might as well delay no further. She tapped on the door.

"It's about time, if I may say so," said a querulous voice from within the room. "Come in. Come in!"

Hillary entered and closed the door behind her. The room smelled musty and closed in. The light was dim, thanks to the heavy draperies that covered the windows. As her eyes accustomed themselves to the grayness, she glanced around the huge room. The furniture was heavy and from another age. The carpets and trimmings were a faded, old-fashioned shade of lavender. In the far corner of the room, stretched out on an ornate daybed and wearing a ruffled lavender dressing gown, rested her patient. An empty wheelchair rested nearby. "I'm over here. Nurse. Make it snappy!"

Hillary let out her breath in a soundless sigh. She had a feeling that "temperamental" was an understatement.

"Good afternoon. Miss Scott. I'm Hillary Holt." She crossed the room in efficient steps, determined to be professional, determined not to let her new patient's reactions make her waver from her judgment about her duties.

She saw the medical folder containing her patient's history laying on the nearby dresser. She picked it up and read the short note the doctor had clipped to the outside.

To the Nurse: I have just heard that you will be arriving today. Here is the information on your patient, and a brief outline of the program I have prescribed for her. Sorry my duties keep me from being on the spot. I'll be by in the morning to meet and confer with you about any problems you may be having with her. And good luck!

Dr. Newburg

Good luck. She had a feeling that she would be needing it!

"How are you feeling today, Miss Scott? I must admit that I've not as yet had time to become familiar with your case history. I received this job on rather short notice."

"So I've heard," sneered the voice from the dim corner of the room. "And aren't I a sight for sore eyes, with these useless legs!" Clumsily she brushed a withered hand over her covered legs and tossed her white head proudly.

Hillary instinctively crossed to the window on the far side of the room. The dimness of the interior was depressing and frustrating. She wanted to see her patient. She pulled back the draperies, and the room was filled with the late afternoon sunlight.

"There. That's much better," Hillary said.

"In whose opinion?" snarled Miss Scott.

The young nurse turned to look at her patient now, more visible in the natural daylight. Her skin was papery and white, an abundance of wrinkles and creases. Her soft, angel-like hair was pulled delicately to the top of her head. She was old, in her late seventies or maybe her eighties. But her eyes contradicted the fact.

For in that face that showed the signs of so many years of life, two bright and very alive eyes stared out and took in all that was going on around them. At the moment she was giving Hillary the most thorough inspection that the girl had ever received.

Hillary stood quietly before her, trying to interpret her gaze.

"Let me tell you something, Nurse. Let us get this straight. I am in charge here. I make the decisions about everything that goes on in this household. You, as well as any other of my employees or guests, will do exactly as I bid. I am not a person to be argued with. And if that situation is not something that you can comply with, then you may pack your bags and go your pretty way. *Am I understood?"*

In her life so far, Hillary had often been barraged by inquisitive lawyers, by pious boarding-school matrons, by demanding nursing instructors, and by temperamental surgeons. She had always held her tongue and her temper, flushing with rage at times, admittedly, but nevertheless refraining from losing her composure and giving vent to an emotional outburst.

Perhaps she was tired on that particular day. Perhaps she was feeling resentment, a deep inner anger for being obligated to take this Eagle's Watch position. Perhaps she just instinctively felt that this woman before her was a personality to be immediately reckoned with, a personality in which she had met her match in stubbornness and strength. But whatever the reason, Hillary opened her mouth and answered the lavender lady sitting so arrogantly before her.

"No, Miss Scott. I'm afraid that you're not understood. First of all, my duty as a nurse is to assist you in every way that I can to make you as comfortable and as healthy as is humanly possible. And while I am in your employ, I cannot answer to any of your wishes that may be detrimental to your health, either in my own opinion, or in the doctor's. Furthermore, I am not a scared little rabbit who is going to hop at your beck and call. If that's what you want, then you've hired the wrong nurse. I am a person, and I insist on being treated with respect. I have taken this position out of a strong feeling of duty, and I fully intend to do the best that I can. But if my work is not satisfactory to you, I'll pack my bags at a moment's notice and be gone before you can give it another thought. And now, are we both understood?"

Hillary knew that her face was burning with a telltale red flush. She was breathless, and her eyes were flashing and angry. And she fully expected the white-haired woman to explode at her outburst.

But she didn't. She just sat there in silence. She sat and stared coolly at the young, freckled redhead who stood proudly in front of her, the nurse who had been sent by her very best friend in the world, Matilda Waverly.

Hillary waited in the deafening silence for the blow to fall, for her employer to send her abruptly away. She was already regretting her impulsive words, if only out of fear that an emotional upset could aggravate her patient's condition.

But Priscilla Scott said nothing for quite some time. And then, very slowly, the traces of a smile began to etch their way on her withered face. Her eyes were dancing.

Then she spoke.

"Now that we've gotten to know each other, Hillary, don't you think it's time we began to work?" She pointed to the doctor's folder that Hillary still clutched in her hand.

Hillary was dumbfounded. She stared into the clear and intelligent eyes of her employer. And slowly, the realization of what was going on dawned on her.

"You just baited me, Priscilla Scott. Didn't you?"

The eyes smiled gleefully back at her.

"And it was such fun! My, I haven't had such a good time in ages." She chuckled in a low, throaty voice.

"But why?"

"To put it bluntly, Hillary Holt, because I had to see who you were. Because I had to see what kind of stuff you were made of. Because I had to make sure you were here on your own accord, an independent person, and not a little snip of a girl who was doing her great-aunt's bidding because her great-aunt held the purse strings."

"But I *am* here to please Miss Matilda," Hillary said honestly.

"Because you feel you owe her something. Which is admirable. But not because you're interested in the rest of her money. Which would not be uncommon. But if that were the case, then you would have cowered before me. You would have done whatever I demanded to stay in her good graces. You wouldn't have dared to risk it all!"

Hillary giggled now and sounded like a young girl. Despite her earlier anger, she felt herself warming toward her patient.

Miss Scott spoke again. "But you blew your cool. And so now I know that Matilda was, as usual, right in her judgment of character. Which is very, very fortunate for me."

Hillary shook her head in disbelief. "Miss Matilda doesn't know anything about me. Miss Scott. I've never even laid eyes on her."

"That just goes to show how little you know, freckled Hillary. She knows just about everything there is to know about you. She's followed your life every step of the way. She cares very much, you know."

"But why has she stayed so far away?" Hillary felt a strange pounding in her ears. Did the answer mean so very much to her?

"She had her reasons, Hillary. She thought it was better that way. And she's usually right, as you will hopefully one day find out. Matilda's a bit of a character. Quite a bit. That's why we're such good friends. But enough of Miss Matilda. We'll have plenty of time to speak of her. Right now, I want to welcome you to Eagle's Watch and tell you how glad I am that you're here. I need you very much, you know."

"I'll help you all that I can."

"I know you will. I'll be open with you and admit something I've never admitted to another soul. This stroke has been quite a shock to me,

Hillary. I feel dependent and vulnerable, a state that doesn't agree with my disposition."

Hillary could well imagine, remembering her employer's sharp tongue on her arrival. "When I read the medical information, I'll have a better view of your condition. I can see that you're the type—well, the type who likes to be on top of things."

"How politely you put it. I'd just say I like to rule over everything in sight. Rather hard to do when you can't stand on your own two feet. By the way, I hope you're a good bird watcher."

A bird watcher? Hillary swallowed. This was all too strange to be true. Was Miss Scott a little senile? It was hard to believe, with those clear, piercing eyes. But still, a bird watcher?

"If you mean eagles, Miss Scott, I must say I didn't see a trace of them as I pulled up."

"Bah, eagles. We'd have to have your head examined if you thought you saw any of those. I haven't seen one for over thirty years. No, it's vultures I'm talking about."

"Vultures!" Hillary cried helplessly. "What vultures?"

"The ones who will be descending on Eagle's Watch very shortly, Nurse Holt. My not-distant-enough relatives, as soon as they receive word of my recent illness. You'll see. Vultures."

"But relatives who care always come around when someone is ill, Miss Scott. Aren't you being just a little unfair to them?"

"I wish I were. But last year, when I suffered a mild angina attack, they flocked from miles around, fluttering like a mob of fools, talking of wills, and legal rights, and driving me crazy. They would have liked to give me a hand into the grave, if you ask me. I'll never forget it. They're a strange group, Nurse Holt. You'll see."

"But I think you're overdoing it. People just aren't that bad, as a rule."

"People don't follow rules when there's a lot of money at stake."

"Personally, I don't give a hoot about money."

"That's why I like you, Hillary. I have a feeling I can trust you."

Hillary could see that her patient was tiring. "You can certainly trust me. Miss Scott. So believe me now when I say you need some rest. I'll go and review the doctor's notes, and then come back after a while."

"Before you go, what do you think of Eagle's Watch?"

Hillary looked into the dark eyes that stared into hers. Only the truth would do.

"Quite honestly, I think it's the strangest and most desolate place I've ever laid eyes upon. But I guess you could say it's intriguing."

The old face was smiling. "Honest girl. I think it's horrible too. I like you, Hillary. What do you think you should call me? Miss Scott sounds a bit formal."

Hillary thought for a moment, feeling a surge of affection for her. "I think you're a little too salty to be called Priscilla. I'd like to call you Scotty. Is that all right? Just between us."

A faraway look came over Priscilla Scott's eyes. "Isn't that a strange coincidence? That's what Matilda always called me." She smiled to herself. "And it's fine, Hillary. Scotty is fine. Now go and do your homework, and let a poor old woman get some much-needed rest."

She closed her eyes, and the nurse tiptoed silently out.

Peeling cozy in the sunny green room next door, Hillary curled up in a big stuffed chair and began to peruse the medical material she had carried with her. The time ticked by; the sun began to sink behind the west wall of the castle.

Priscilla Scott was eighty-four years old. Her medical history was generally one of a relatively healthy woman, aside from the usual problems that often accompany the later years of life. Her joints worked well, her digestion had been excellent. Her eyes occasionally gave her problems, she tired easily.

She suffered from a minor case of angina pectoris, an ailment of the heart which was carefully controlled by the administration of nitroglycerin tablets at the onset of an attack. Since her first attack, over a year ago, she had rarely had any signs or symptoms, an indication that the condition was fairly well under control. Hillary knew that individuals with angina could often live full and active lives for years and years, taking the proper precautions and having good medical supervision.

The stroke that had occurred a few weeks ago had been a relatively minor one. It had not affected her speech or her vision, as is so often the case. Her right side had been weakened, the coordination in her arm and leg had suffered from the attack, and the right side of her face showed the slightest trace of a droop. Her left side had been unaffected except for a lingering tiredness from her body's ordeal.

She had returned from the hospital only the day before, and had been temporarily cared for by a very nervous Mrs. Raymond.

Her vital signs were listed as strong, her pulse, blood pressure, and temperature showed that she was doing well. The doctor had prescribed an extensive rehabilitation program for her, containing exercises and activities to gradually increase the overall strength in her body, and to redevelop the coordination lost in her right limbs.

Hillary thought back over the months she had spent on the wards of the city hospital during her training, months that she had worked with several patients who had suffered similar tragedies. In some severe cases, the stroke victims had never been able to return to any semblance of normal health. Some patients had been very old, some had been amazingly young. And some, like Priscilla Scott, had had the good fortune to have a better than fair chance of regaining all of the ground that they had lost. Given a strong will—there was no doubt that Scotty possessed that—and the determination to do a lot of hard work, she could recuperate. She would walk again and be released from the wheelchair that confined her.

Stroke patients often remained at the hospital for their physical therapy, working for weeks, even months, on the elaborate equipment that was provided. But Priscilla Scott had returned home. Hillary suppressed a giggle, sure that she knew why. She could just imagine the proud white head bobbing defiantly, berating and terrorizing the nurses and orderlies on the hospital floor, her arrogant voice refusing abruptly to follow their orders, refusing to fit into their daily system. Hillary could just imagine her dealing with the therapists who would try to bend her will.

Hillary had seen a good many patients in her day, and some had been quite difficult to work with. But none, she knew, could hold a candle to Priscilla Scott! The staff had probably been more than relieved when Dr. Newburg had removed her from their care.

And now she was Hillary's patient. Hillary smiled to herself. Scotty was going to get better. They would have storms and rages most probably. But she would ultimately do what she had to do to get better, because she had met her match in stubbornness in Hillary Holt. The young nurse hadn't wanted this position, to be sure, but now she was here and she was determined to succeed. And she liked Scotty. She closed the folder firmly and answered the knock on her door.

The clock on her dresser chimed six times. Mrs. Raymond stood in the doorway and immediately began to rattle off her message.

"I've come to inform you of the meal arrangements, Nurse Holt. Tonight I will bring you a tray in your room. Breakfast tomorrow will also be served in this way. The family will be arriving throughout the day tomorrow, and from then on, meals will be at eight, twelve, and eight, promptly, in the dining room downstairs. You are expected to join the family for meals, and to give them a report of Miss Scott's condition."

"And what of Miss Scott? Will she be joining us?"

Mrs. Raymond looked at her in confusion. It was the first human emotion that Hillary had seen in her.

"Miss Scott seems to prefer staying in her room, and when I spoke to the family on the telephone, they seemed to think that was best."

"But that isn't normally what she'd do?"

"No. She's one who usually likes to well, be in charge. I'm not quite sure what to do..."

"Perhaps you could serve my tray along with Miss Scott's in her room this evening, and I'll speak to her about it."

She was not going to let Scotty withdraw from the world. She was going to take the bull by the horns.

The little housekeeper looked at her out of the corner of her eye. It was plain to see that she disliked Hillary.

"Whatever you say, I suppose. But I'm too busy to think about it. This place has to be as clean as a whistle, with the family arriving tomorrow, and I've got only Annie, the cook, in the kitchen, and a new maid who's to arrive tomorrow." She shook her head in disgust.

"How many of the family will be coming?"

"All four of them. And it'll seem like a hundred. They expect the best, I don't mind telling you. And they don't hesitate to complain. So I've got to get back to work. And I've got no time to cater to the likes of you."

She strutted off importantly to tackle her many tasks, leaving Hillary staring after her, feeling undeserving of the woman's obvious dislike.

Chapter 3

"Nurse Holt can assist me with my dinner, Mrs. Raymond," Scotty barked a few moments later. "I don't need the likes of you hovering about me so." She brushed away the housekeeper, who was setting up the meal trays, and the little woman left the room with her head bowed low. She was a picture of servitude at the moment, of humility and meekness, except for the long, dark look that she sent like a dagger to Hillary. Again Hillary could read the angry dislike in her birdlike face, and with a sinking sensation, she wondered why the little housekeeper resented her.

Because she would be working so closely with Miss Scott? Jealousy? Remembering Scotty's sharp tone, she considered that unlikely. But still, for some reason, the dislike was there.

After Hillary finished checking Scotty's pulse and blood pressure, charting them carefully in the doctor's file, they sat and consumed their meal together.

Scotty ate her specially prepared dinner with the expected number of complaints, Hillary's experienced hand assisting her to guide the small spoonfuls of pureed food to her mouth.

"According to the doctor's report, you're in pretty good shape, Scotty."

"That old codger. It just goes to show how little he knows. If I'm in such tremendous condition, why am I confined to this chair? Why aren't I up walking around?"

Hillary looked straight into her eyes. "Because you haven't been trying hard enough. You've given up. But that will change now."

"We'll see about that," Scotty began crossly, but then a wrinkled grin crept across her pale face. "On second thought, I have a feeling that I'm just wasting my energy by arguing with you, Hillary Holt. I wouldn't want to wager on who was more stubborn! So we'll try it your way, but don't you go spreading it around that I'm being cooperative. I happen to take pride in my bristly reputation."

Hillary laughed easily. "That's fine, Scotty. I'll never breathe a word to a soul that you are not the fire-breathing dragon of Eagle's Watch. Just so you work hard for me, and get well. We'll start tomorrow morning, when you're well rested."

They sat together for the next few hours, enjoying each other's company, and Hillary learned a bit about the history of Eagle's Watch.

It had been built almost one hundred fifty years before, its stones shipped laboriously across the ocean and assembled on the shores of Maine, almost a duplicate of an ancient castle that had stood solidly in Great Britain for a number of centuries. Eagle's Watch was smaller and sported many more windows than its predecessor, whose thick walls had had to protect the castle from the somewhat barbarous world in medieval times. But its square, solid design strongly echoed those times gone by.

More recently, an electrical system and complete plumbing had been installed, bringing the conveniences of modern living to the place. But much of the decoration of the interior of the castle remained as it had for generations of the Scott family, passing down to each heir its long history and tradition.

Priscilla Scott, self-admittedly a character from her earliest days, had been the first Scott to rebel. She had not spent much of her time within the thick walls, and when she was present, she had made an effort to throw off the gloomy atmosphere that hung over the place. She had redecorated a few rooms in a more modern style, and had gone about her life in her usual self-reliant way.

She was the first in the long chain of American Scotts who had not married and produced an heir.

"That's what the family is so excited about," she said. "They know I can will the entire family fortune away on a moment's whim, and so they want to be certain that they're all in the running."

"This place is so large. I imagine it's worth quite a lot."

"No, no, my dear, you're very off base. This castle is a white elephant, a relic from another age. Impractical, to say the least, except as a museum or monument or some such thing. But there is Scott family money tied up in a variety of holdings, and the land that surrounds the estate is practically priceless. The estate takes in hundreds of acres, ripe for development, for housing projects and resorts. But the land will stay as it is, if I have anything to say about it.

"The whole estate belongs to me, and I'll do with it as I please. I have no respect for those who grovel for money, as if it were the hub of the universe. It has to be kept in perspective. There are a lot more important things in life than money. Remember that, Hillary."

Scotty closed her eyes and leaned her head back, drifting into a world of memories, stories that were absorbed eagerly by Hillary's waiting ears.

She had been an only child of wealthy parents, parents who had tried to shield her from the world outside, to keep her from associating with what they considered the "riffraff" of life. But Scotty had been too full of curiosity and energy to follow their commands.

She had run away from home at the ripe old age of seventeen, with her best childhood friend, Matilda. Hillary's great-aunt!

Together they had traveled to Europe, a daring escapade for unchaperoned girls in that era, and had weathered a number of scrapes and predicaments as they had traveled through life. Matilda had decided to settle in London, and Priscilla had returned finally to her family in Maine. She had never stayed long within the thick stone walls of Eagle's Watch, crisscrossing the ocean constantly to see the world and to visit Matilda, until her last bout of illness had left her confined.

Priscilla's parents had died, leaving her the grand inheritance of Eagle's Watch. She had never married, never been willing to settle down in one place for quiet family life. And now, very alone, she was confined to a chair in the old stone castle.

"Do I detect a note of self-pity?" asked Hillary with a slight smile.

"From me! Good heavens, child!" Scotty barked in self-defense. "Never."

"There is no reason for you to spend the rest of your days cooped up within these four walls, you know, and I'm not going to allow you to. You act as though you've resigned from the world, Priscilla Scott, hiding away up in this dark room.

"Mrs. Raymond says that the family will be arriving during the day tomorrow, so you might as well be ready to come downstairs to take over your role of mistress here. They may not be your favorite people, but they are people nonetheless."

"Debatable."

"Don't be impossible."

"But I can't go downstairs. The wheelchair—"

"I'll arrange for another one to be ready downstairs. Mr. Raymond can carry you up and down as you desire."

"Carried up and down! Like a sack of potatoes! I'd rather die." She shook her proud head.

"Nonsense. It's a small price to pay for your independence. And it won't be for long. I have every intention of getting you up on your feet again."

Scotty's eyes were glistening with tears. "I'll have to think about it."

Hillary looked at her slyly, acutely sensitive to the flood of fears and inadequacies that she was feeling. She had to help her to be strong. She took a deep breath and began.

"I find it hard to believe that the woman I see sitting before me is the same character that I've just been hearing tales about. It seems to me that a girl who would dare to cross the ocean unescorted would certainly dare to meet a few hovering relatives, even ones with their hands out. It's sad to see you defeated like that."

"Defeated!" roared the old woman, her eyes burning. "Don't you dare say that to me. No one can defeat Priscilla Scott. Not relatives. Not this wheelchair. Please inform Mrs. Raymond that lunch will be served in the dining room tomorrow. And I will be there." Her voice was sharp, proud.

"I just thought you might, Scotty," said Hillary with a twinkle in her green eyes. "I'll go see about the chair." She turned to go out of the room.

"Hillary?"

She turned to face Scotty once again, "Yes?"

"Thanks."

The hour came for Hillary to help her patient to prepare for the night ahead. She assisted her in her nightly bathing routines and helped her to slip a freshly laundered night dress over her head.

Hillary brushed the long white hair with deft, easy strokes and braided it into a thick plait that hung down her back.

When Scotty was ready to retire, she tucked her carefully into the large waiting bed. She looked small, propped against the fluffy pillows, covered with the downy comforter that adorned the bed.

"I'll see you first thing in the morning, Scotty," she said as she did a last-minute check of her patient's vital signs and added the data to the chart. Her condition was strong and stable. "I'll be in during the night to make sure you're doing well."

"Like the sadistic nurses at the hospital who get some morbid delight in shining a light into your eyes?"

"You won't even know I'm here, you grouch. By the way, do you mind if I wander about and give myself a tour of the castle? I can't help but be curious about it."

"Help yourself. But take a flashlight, since the sun is down. There is electricity throughout, but the lightbulbs probably need to be replaced in spots. I can't say I've paid much attention to most of the place."

"Well, if I'm not back by morning, send out a search party," Hillary teased.

"If you're lucky, perhaps Percival will accompany you on your rounds. He knows his way around here best of anyone."

Percival? Was there someone else in the house that she had yet to meet?

Scotty gave an amused chuckle.

"Percival would no doubt consider himself the most important member of the household, and when you do run into him, you will find your life easier if you don't disillusion him."

"And where will I find Percival?"

"Oh, you won't find him, he'll find you. You see, Percival is a cat. A distinguished, proud, and extremely arrogant beast if I ever saw one. Reminds me a bit of myself, he does. He's large, and black as midnight itself. I do hope he can tolerate you to a greater extent than he can that sour-faced Mrs. Raymond. She's constantly trying to bend his will, and it's a hopeless task. He gives her a run for the money. Very entertaining."

She chuckled quietly as she settled down to sleep, and Hillary tiptoed silently out, closing the door softly behind her.

She stopped briefly in her room and retrieved a flashlight from the shelf in the bathroom closet. She had just stepped into the hallway when the sound of a ruckus greeted her ears.

"Get out of here, you no-good cat!" Mrs. Raymond's exasperated voice traveled up the long stairway. Hillary looked over the railing in time to see the angry little housekeeper scurry across the foyer below, broom in hand, chasing the sleek cat who forever remained a few paces in front of her.

In frustration, Mrs. Raymond gave up the chase and headed back in the direction from which she had come. The cat sauntered proudly up the stairs toward Hillary, a distinctly satisfied look on his face.

"Well, hello, Sir Percival," Hillary addressed him softly as he approached. With his black, sleek coat, he certainly had a majestic appearance. "I can see you had a marvelous time baiting Mrs. Raymond down there. Would you care to take me on a tour of the castle?"

He turned up his nose and ignored her, true to his character. Hillary laughed and started down the long flight of stairs to begin her exploration of the castle. Percival followed a respectable distance behind.

Along the wall as she descended, she found the life-size family portraits of the past members of the Scott family, portraits that she had quickly admired upon her arrival at Eagle's Watch. They hung so solemnly in their heavy gilt frames, the latest being a hard-faced man garbed in a stately suit, most probably Priscilla's long dead father. Each frame reached back into time, with the earliest dated nearly one hundred fifty years before—the first American Scott, who was responsible for the erection of Eagle's Watch. She studied the wide variety of costume, some in shiny buttoned uniforms from the various wars, some in the grand finery that was proudly worn by the gentlemen of the times.

All in all, they were a sober lot, with eyes cool and piercing, even from the canvas, and while Hillary found them intriguing to study, she found them hard to identify with the present mistress of Eagle's Watch.

She reached the bottom of the staircase, and the spacious foyer, her feet softly contacting the polished stoned floor in her rubber-soled nursing shoes. The light was very dim and no one was in sight. Percival rubbed affectionately against her leg, and she found herself glad for his unpredictable company.

The castle, she soon discovered, was laid out in a huge square, its massive wings completely enclosing a small inner courtyard that sat in the center, completely protected from the outside world, open only to the sky above. There were two floors in the castle, with the two high turrets that towered above them. The basement, or "dungeon," that had sat morbidly beneath the original castle across the ocean, had been left out of the design of the Scott family estate, and Eagle's Watch sat firmly on top of solid rock.

She moved to the right of the foyer, swinging open a heavy door and passing quickly through it.

She found herself in the living room. Here, signs of Scotty's up-to-date decorating showed through, though the great height of the ceilings and the squareness of the deep-set windows still proclaimed the castlelike aura of the place. But the furniture was well loved and comfortable looking; the room had a lived in feeling. Hillary was beginning to chide herself for the misgivings she had first had. Both her own room and the living room were normal, happy rooms, far from the outlandish imaginings her mind had expected.

But as she moved into the hallway, and traveled to the next room in the wing, her doubts returned. Commonly called a drawing room, its stiff formality seemed forbidding. She crossed the intricate Persian rug and lighted a lamp to see more clearly. There were brocade chairs, placed alongside daintily carved end tables of some exotic wood, unfamiliar to Hillary by name, though their great worth was apparent. The elaborate furniture, the crystal chandeliers, all added to the untouchable air of antiquity that permeated the room. She felt like an intruder, a trespasser in a room that didn't welcome human occupation.

She looked furtively around, not quite able to shake the feeling that she was unwelcome in the room. It was ridiculous, she knew. It was only a room, and she had been given Scotty's permission to explore. Still, she found herself eager to move on.

Next she followed the long hallway to a huge archway that supported a pair of ornate doors. When she swung them open, she was greeted by an overwhelming darkness.

She switched her flashlight on quickly, as her hand sought along the nearby wall for a lightswitch. The room sprang to life, and Hillary's eyes widened in awe.

She had found the ballroom of the castle, and it was truly magnificent. The windows were heavily covered with elegant brocade draperies, their golden weave glimmering richly. Graceful gilt chairs lined the long walls; the floor was covered with inlaid tiles. There was an attractive dais at one end of the huge room, and Hillary could just imagine the tuxedoed orchestra that must have perched upon it for so many of the Scott family celebrations.

The chandeliers on the ceiling glittered with light, and Hillary found herself envisioning the stately couples of earlier times, spinning around the graceful floor together, moving to the happy music, dresses flowing around them, their curled hair piled high. She stood alone in the midst of all her imagined splendor for several minutes, trying to envision herself in the conjured dream.

Percival's peevish yowl brought her abruptly back to the present, amazed at the romantic and exhilarating thoughts that had affected her so. Really, what was this place doing to her?

She found the hallway windows that looked out onto the enclosed garden, a little courtyard showing signs of neglect and decay. It most probably came far down on the list of priorities in a place such as this, with only Mr. Raymond to tend to the upkeep. But it was a shame, for it seemed a peaceful and thought- provoking place.

Two marble cherubs looked sprightly in now-dry fountains, encrusted with moss and the signs of time. Hillary made a mental note to explore it more fully when she had more than the stolen light from the hallway windows and a small hand-held flashlight to cast light into it.

The great hall in the castle made a turn to the left and traveled along the rear wing of the castle. There were a number of smaller rooms, a sitting room, laundry room, utility areas. On the fourth side of the castle, she found the large and extremely well-arranged kitchen, appliances and counters gleaming brightly in the overhead light. The pantry was well stocked. The small servants' eating area was rather bleak and cold. There was no one to be seen.

Coming closer to the front of the castle, she found the formal dining room, its long oval table sitting squarely in the center, its highbacked chairs adding to the regal appearance. The high ceiling and coldness of the walls made even the huge table seem dwarfed. The great stone fireplace stood empty and cold in the summer evening.

The last room she found on the first floor was a book-filled study, its walls lined high with extensive shelves of musty-smelling volumes. A heavy antique desk commanded the room, demanding silence, demanding respect. She was eager to slip through its solemness to the doorway beyond. She found herself once again in the front foyer.

She had traveled completely around the square that was the main floor of the castle, and her emotions were mixed ones. It belonged to another age, another life, despite Scotty's attempts to modernize a few of the rooms. No wonder Scotty had never rightfully been able to call it "home."

Hillary moved up the grand staircase to the upper floor, not really anxious to see more of the castle's massiveness, but nevertheless feeling compelled to get it over with. Percival had disappeared.

She flicked the light switches in the hallway as she moved along, trying not to notice the eeriness of the shadows that were cast.

Besides the rooms occupied by herself and Scotty, there were a number of other dramatic bedrooms, as regal as they were outdated, but freshly cleaned and polished for the soon arriving family members. Along the back wing, she opened door after door of empty bedrooms, not as elegant as those in the family wing, but well furnished and definitely striking. In its active times. Eagle's Watch could have housed dozens of guests without turning a hair.

She was excited when she found the first doorway to one of the turrets. The stairway crept ambitiously upward, winding around and around until the high room at the top was reached.

With delighted surprise, she found that the high circular room with its magnificent panoramic view of the moonlit ocean, was, in fact, a sculptor's studio. A well-used artist's table showed the signs of hours of dedicated work. Long, low shelving showed some of the products in various stages of completion. Hillary was awed by the beauty of the work. From lumps of heavy gray clay, the artist's hands had brought forth so much beauty-intricate and realistic statues of the woodland creatures that scurried through the pines along the coast, graceful, flowing abstracts that seemed to hover in their places on the shelves. Truly beautiful.

But the room showed no sign of current occupation, she realized with a closer inspection. A fine mist of dust coated the table and shelves. The remaining clay in its barrel by the doorway was hardened and cracked. As if the artist had been prevented from returning to this haven of creativity. Scotty?

Hillary felt a tinge of excitement at the thought. Had Scotty been the artist who had created with such talent? Had her stroke prevented her from going on? It seemed right somehow, for someone like Scotty to be the recipient of such an artistic gift. And if the work had stopped because of her physical disabilities, it was very possible that she would begin one day again. Hillary's mind was turning as she left the turret behind.

She wandered slowly through the rear quarters of the castle, meandering through the sometimes darkened rooms with her thoughts fixed elsewhere. So many rooms!

It seemed a pity to have them standing empty and unused. She found the second turret approximately where she had expected it to be, symmetrically even with the first tower on the opposite side of the castle. She opened the door soundlessly and crept up the darkened stairs. She turned on the lightswitch, but the beam that was thrown on the steps was a weak one. Up and up she went, curious as to what this turret held.

And when she found out, she was almost as surprised as she had been when she had discovered the first turret room, though certainly not as pleasantly so.

In the dim light, she could see shapes lining the curved walls of stone and glass. The windows were bare, but the night was dark outside, and so no additional moonlight filtered in through the glass to aid her straining eyes.

Was the room full of people? She gulped in fear, ready to start and tear down the winding stairway behind her. But her pulse slowly returned to normal as she stared more deeply into the shadows.

Armor! The room was lined with several full suits of ancient armor, standing tall and proud in their darkened corner of the castle, almost as if they possessed souls of their own. In style, each differed greatly. Some were solid and ornate, others covered with chain mail. She passed the beam of her flashlight over each and noticed the gleam that reflected off their surfaces. The relics stood here, high in the castle turret, in the most deserted wing of the entire building, a building empty except for an ailing old woman and a few overworked servants.

But the armor was far from neglected. Obviously, it was well taken care of. And who was responsible for that painstaking effort? It made no sense.

And then she heard it.

At first, she had supposed that the slight noise she had picked up had come from Percival, following her at a distance. But the sound was repeated, again and again. Someone was walking through the corridor at the bottom of the turret steps. Someone's definite footsteps were echoing soundly on the stone floor, and getting clearer and closer with each step.

She stood petrified. Who was it?

She crossed the turret room instinctively to one of the tallest suits of armor. As forbidding as it had appeared only seconds before, it suddenly became a haven, a protector. She darted behind it, hiding. For the footsteps were now climbing the steps, and their owner would be appearing at the top of the flight in a very few seconds' time.

Why was she filled with this unreasonable fear, this sudden panic that was enveloping her, making her breath come rapidly, making the back of her neck prickle as she stood in the darkness? I his crazy place had unsettled her so drastically. Had Scotty's fears of "vultures" and her own overworked imagination colored her ability to think clearly?

After all, it was probably Mrs. Raymond, or even Mr. Raymond, trying to find her, to give her a message, to show her around. There were a million normal reasons why someone might be seeking her out. She was being ridiculous in her fright.

She was almost ready to step forward into the slight beam of light that filtered into the turret room, ashamed to admit her slip of reason, ready to laugh at her sudden attack of suspicion. But just as she was putting her foot out from behind the polished armor, a dark head appeared at the top of the stairway. It was not Mrs. Raymond, it was not Mr. Raymond.

Indeed, the figure that climbed the last few steps, slowly and quietly, was a person she had never seen before. The fear was stuck in her throat again. Her heart was pounding with great intensity.

What should she do?

The dark figure spoke.

"Now isn't that the strangest thing? Where the heck did she get to? Nurse Holt? Nurse Holt, where are you?"

His voice was young and cheerful and light. Somehow it didn't fit the terrifying image she had conjured up of her pursuer. She took a deep breath and stepped out from her shadowy hideout.

"I'm right here," she said quietly. "Why are you following me?" Her voice was cool and calm, hut her heart was still hammering at a ferocious pace. She didn't like this place. She didn't like the things it did to her mind.

"Just playing detective. I guess. I suppose you're wondering who the heck I am."

"Good deduction, Sherlock." Her green eyes stared defiantly into his.

"Oh, a feisty one. I like that. Well, for starters, I'm Mitchell Morrison, aged twenty-six, most distant relative of the wonder-witch who owns this mausoleum. My grandmother was her cousin. Don't ask me to tell you what relation that makes me. I just call myself a distant relative. And you are Hillary Holt, the new Florence Nightingale of Eagle's Watch. So now we've been introduced. Nice to meet you."

His attitude was light and flip, and Hillary wasn't at all sure that the feeling was mutual.

"I thought the family was arriving tomorrow."

"So we are, formally, that is. The other three will arrive in fashion, late in the morning, I'd guess. But I got an offer of a lift most of the way here from New York, so I grabbed it. Some of us find it necessary to watch our expenses, you know. But I didn't want to bother Aunt Priscilla with my change of plans. She thinks I'm an irresponsible devil. So I just settled in and thought I'd announce myself in the morning. Old Mrs. Raymond took care of everything. Have you run into her yet?" His eyes were twinkling.

"Run into is exactly what I've done. We don't exactly get along, for some reason."

"Don't mind Mrs. Raymond," he said, throwing his head back with a laugh. She noticed his even white teeth, his wavy, longish hair, his dark clear eyes. He really was quite handsome when he laughed.

"Mrs. Raymond and I get on famously. I'm not here often, but when I am, she gives me the royal treatment. But it doesn't surprise me that you don't get the same. Her son, Tony, is about my age, and he was always the apple of her eye. But about three years ago, he ran off with a spritely little redhead, much to his parents' undying dismay.

"Of course, they blamed it all on the 'willful' girl, but I'll tell you this, old Tony was hooked on her. She was something else. I don't blame him at all, no matter how long it lasts.

"But Mrs. Raymond says I remind her of her dear boy, and so she coddles me something awful. Which I love."

He reached out to Hillary and touched her red hair. "And with that crop of red hair, Hillary, there's no doubt whom you'll remind her of. Best to lock your door at night!"

They laughed then, and Hillary finally relaxed. They moved down the winding stairway and into the better light of the corridor below.

"It was easy to find you, Hillary," Mitchell said as he turned off the lightswitch behind them. "You left quite a trail of lights."

Hillary felt her face flush with color. How thoughtlessly she had wandered through almost every room of the castle, turning on lights along the way to dispel the gloom and chase the shadows from the corners, leaving them on behind her. Her cheeks turned red with embarrassment.

But her dismay only made Mitchell laugh harder. "Yes, as I came around the last corner of the drive, I thought the place had finally gone up in flames. I must say I've never seen it so lit up before. But never fear, I followed behind you and dutifully turned them all off."

They passed through the servants' wing, where the sounds of living could be heard, the tinny sound of a radio and quiet voices, as the Raymonds and Annie, the cook, settled in for their evening.

They emerged at the top of the main stairway. The rest of the house stood silently. Only the rumble of the nearby waves beat rhythmically on the shoreline.

"Well, thank you for saving my face by turning off the lights." Hillary offered at the door to her room. "I think I'd have rather died that go through this place again tonight."

"Not too impressed, huh?"

"Impressed is not the word. Overwhelmed, perhaps. It's so full of history and tradition from the past. But as a house, as a home—"

"I know exactly what you mean," he said lightly. "You'd have to be slightly off your rocker to enjoy inhabiting a place like this. But I sure wouldn't mind inheriting the whole works." There was a twinkle in his eye. "And now I'll leave you, fair damsel of the castle, to get your beauty rest. Not that you need it, of course. Don't say anything to Aunt Priscilla about me being here ahead of schedule, okay? I want to stay on her good side, if it's possible to find one!"

She didn't answer him, but he took her silence for agreement.

"I'm glad you're here, Hillary," he said, looking deeply into her green eyes. "You have a lot of spunk. I knew as soon as Mrs. Raymond said you'd taken off to go through the castle at night, you must be one of the stouthearted ones, as they say."

"Mrs. Raymond knew I'd gone through the castle?" Hillary asked in surprise. She'd seen no sign of the bristly little housekeeper in her wanderings.

"Don't fool yourself, Hillary. You can get the impression that no one knows anything that is going on around this huge place, but it's rarely the truth. The walls have eyes, I think.

"And so, for tonight, I'll say farewell, my lady. My room is right across the hall, in case you should need my help to slay a dragon or some other gallant deed during the night."

He bowed with a flourish and kissed Hillary's hand, disappearing into the room across the hall with his laughing eyes and easygoing nature. And Hillary Holt felt very funny inside.
* * *

She climbed out of her uniform and got herself ready for bed in the attractive green room that was now hers. She climbed between the cool sheets of the huge bed and settled down for a much needed sleep. But it didn't come right away.

The day had been a long and eventful one for her. To find a place such as Eagle's Watch after her day-long journey had been enough of a shock. To have met and appreciated the unbreakable spirit of Priscilla Scott was excitement in itself, set in the gloom and somehow mysterious aura that hovered over the huge stone place.

But finally, her sudden reaction to the man who was Mitchell Morrison was a very unsettling experience. She put a hand up to her red hair, where he had touched it so casually in the far-off turret room. He had made her stomach light and flighty.

And his kiss on her hand, a purely theatrical one from his point of view, had set her heart to pounding with a newfound excitement.

And these reactions were very strange to her. In nursing school, she had driven herself with the compulsion to succeed in the field of medicine. She had built a barrier around herself, not unlike the medieval suits of armor that stood in the castle. She had worked every waking hour on her dream, and had never allowed herself to become close to anyone she came into contact with. She stood alone.

She never bothered with the lighthearted crushes and interpersonal games that so many of her classmates had thrived on. Indeed, she looked upon their moonings as childish, immature. And now she was not so sure. Was she so different from them, after all? To have enjoyed the company of the young man she just met, a man she didn't really even know, and of whom she probably wouldn't even approve. After all, wasn't he self-admittedly here to be in Scotty's good graces? Grovelers, she called them.

Hillary sighed and pulled the covers tightly around her. She had a feeling that there was much she needed to learn about life. Her life had changed drastically in the past few days. She was having to face ideas and situations that she had had no experience with. How would she do?

She felt a flutter of anticipation in her stomach at the thought. She closed her eyes and drifted into a restful sleep, eager to see what tomorrow would bring at Eagle's Watch.

Chapter 4

Hillary awakened soundlessly in the middle of the night to make a check on her patient's condition, and found her sleeping well. When she returned to her own bed, she slept until the insistent clamor of her alarm clock announced that the hour had arrived to begin a new day.

It was early, and the sun was casting a pinkish glow to all she could see from her bedroom window. From the second floor, high above the rocks and crashing waves below, she was filled with a kind of awesome respect for the power of nature unleashed in the foamy tide.

She bathed and dressed quickly, feeling eager to begin the therapy program that would bring Scotty closer to recovery. She was spotlessly dressed, hair in place, looking cleanly scrubbed and fresh when Mrs. Raymond arrived with the breakfast tray. She greeted the woman cheerfully, ignoring the icy silence she received in return, and thankfully accepted the steaming platter of eggs, bacon, and toast. She was ravenous.

Scotty was propped up in bed when Hillary arrived a short while later, and she was wearing an expectant look on her face. It confirmed Hillary's instincts that she was more than ready to face the steps that she would need to take to improve her physical condition.

"Good morning, Scotty," she said gaily as she took her blood pressure, pulse, and temperature.

All were normal. She gave her her daily dose of digoxin, a medication prescribed by the doctor in the medical report, necessary to control her heart condition.

The next half hour passed quickly as Hillary helped Scotty to bathe and dress for the day, voicing encouragement as she eased her patient into her waiting wheelchair.

"Of course, the path ahead of you will be a strenuous one, Scotty. You'll need to rest often while we work on your recuperation. But since you can sit up so well, and move your arms a bit, I see no reason to doubt that you'll be up and around again."

She saw the pain of fear in Scotty's eyes. "I do hope you are right, Hillary. I really do. I have to admit to you that I've never felt so desperate and worthless in my entire life. But I'm starting to hope again, now that you're here. I trust you." Her eyes began to regain their teasing glimmer. "Though why, I don't know. But I'll work hard, you'll see. Much harder than I did for those silly pampered therapists in the hospital. My, I certainly did shake things up around there!"

"I can just imagine. And it's a good thing you didn't have me as your nurse then. I may have assisted you out a window." She delighted in

Scotty's chuckle as she finished pinning the soft white hair to the top of her head.

"Yes, we're a good match, Hillary Holt."

Mrs. Raymond arrived to announce the arrival of Dr. Newburg. He followed the black-clad housekeeper into the room and greeted Scotty with a grunt.

"Making trouble Priscilla?"

Mrs. Raymond exited quietly. Hillary looked at the aged physician who stood before her. His hair was sparse and ruffled, his suit a bit unkempt. Despite the morning hour, he had the distinct look of needing a good sleep, which she soon found out was very true.

"Spent the better part of the night taking care of old Mr. Dolson down in town, Priscilla. He's taken another bad turn and I'm afraid it looks pretty bad. So don't give me any of your usual grief, woman, as I'm not in the mood to benefit by it. I've got sicker patients than you to take care of, and ones who are trying to get well. Hello, Nurse Holt," he said in an offhand way, as if he had known her for weeks.

"This is the not-so-famous Dr. Newburg, Hillary, kindly physician to all for miles and miles around." Scotty's voice was teasing, but for once, kindly. "Overworked and underpaid, eh, Doc? And he's been driving himself to drink, trying to convince me to take part in his schemes for rehabilitating me. To which I've put up quite a resistance, to date. You'll be glad to know, Dr. Newburg, that Hillary has convinced me to go along with your plan, so I hope I won't be on your overloaded patient list for long."

"She did?" he said in stark amazement. He turned and looked at Hillary intently. His eyes held respect and a bit of wonder. "And how did she do that?"

"Coercion. The little snip threatened to toss me out a window."

Dr. Newburg laughed heartily, and he looked quite a bit younger, his face momentarily relieved of the tension and tiredness that had filled it before. "I should have thought of that myself."

He quickly went over the data that Hillary had collected in her few hours of association with her patient, and was happy to see that Priscilla was strong and steady, as well as impressed with Hillary's efficiency and accuracy.

They left Scotty for a few moments to go down to the living room to consult about the physical therapy program that Scotty would begin.

"By the way, Hillary," Scotty said slyly as the doctor and nurse went out the door. "If you should run into that no-good relative, Mitchell Morrison, this morning, tell him I hope he had a restful sleep last night."

Hillary giggled. Even hidden up here in her closed room, away from the daily happenings of Eagle's Watch, while feeling depressed and unhappy and unable to cope with the drastic changes that her own life had undergone, Scotty was clever, observant, wise enough to know exactly what was going on.

She was definitely one of a kind.

The living room on the first floor was deserted when Hillary and Dr. Newburg sat down in two comfortable chairs to go over the facts of Priscilla Scott's case.

Her heart condition was controlled by a daily dose of digoxin, to be given each morning, as it had been today. If the symptoms of angina pectoris were to recur, causing a definite pain in the heart region of the chest, Hillary was to administer two tablets of nitroglycerin immediately, to be dissolved under the patient's tongue. Good care and protection from stressful situations would greatly lessen any chance that these dangerous warning signs would recur.

The therapy for recovery from the stroke was much as Hillary had expected. Since the damage done had not been too extensive, and since the initial therapy Scotty had received in the hospital had enabled her to progress to the point where she could sit up with assistance, (though far from willingly, the doctor chuckled, thinking of the headaches she had caused during her stay in the hospital), she was ready to begin an extensive exercise program.

Her right limbs had been affected, showing that the stroke had occurred in the left sector of the brain. Her left arm was movable, though weakened from the general strain on her body, her left leg the same. There was a slight droop to the right side of her face, but the speech center had not been affected.

Hillary would have to be sure that her patient received no sedation, nor consumed any liquor during her recuperation. Her meals, as Mrs. Raymond and the cook had been instructed, were to be soft and easily digestible.

The exercise program the doctor prescribed was one that began with passive movement, where Hillary would rhythmically move Scotty's limbs back and forth, back and forth, to redevelop the nerve and muscle patterns that had been lost with the stroke. He carefully described the series of motions that she would go through each session, gradually expanding in number as her strength returned.

The vital signs had to be diligently checked for any sign of overwork or relapse. The blood pressure must remain normal, the pulse regular, as uneven signs could indicate undue stress on the heart. A rising temperature would be a warning, as would rapid breathing or uneven dilation of the pupils in the eyes.

All in all, Hillary felt that her job was relatively easy. She was to assist her patient in the recovery process, while carefully monitoring the response of her body, making sure that all of her vital signs were under control.

Not a mind-shattering task, she had to admit, after her heady dreams of surgical nursing at a prestigious hospital. But it would be an interesting change of pace, and a chance to help Scotty recover some of the life that she felt she had lost. And for some reason, that was very important to her.

She listened carefully to the elderly doctor and learned about him as she learned about her patient. He knew Scotty well, indeed. Theirs had been a relationship that went back for many, many years.

"She acts like a tough old bird," he said, running a tired hand through his unkempt gray hair. "But her heart's really in the right place, once you get to know her. I guess I don't have to tell you that, from what I've seen." He looked at Hillary with a questioning glance. "You seem to have her in the palm of your hand."

Hillary laughed. "I don't think either of us will ever see the day when Priscilla Scott is in the palm of anyone's hand, Doctor. It seems to me she has a very definite mind of her own."

"Well, that's true, as you say." He began stacking up the medical papers laid out before them, and returned them to the file. "I can't help but worry that someone will get the better of her, make her do something that may not be in her best interest. She's getting old. And she's worth a lot, that woman up there."

"So I've heard."

"Hmm. Well, I've got to get going. Have a full schedule today, and I've got to stop home to clean myself up before I hit the road again. I'm getting old myself, I guess. I'm getting to the point where I'd much rather do research. It'll be good to know you're here, Nurse Holt. Takes the pressure off me coming up this way every day. I'll stop by a few times a week, to check out on the progress, and of course you can always reach me by phone. The answering service usually knows which direction I'm heading in, and they can track me down."

He looked at Hillary for a moment.

"Was there something else. Dr. Newburg?"

"Matter of fact, I did have one more question. I was wondering what a young girl like you was doing with a job like this, way out here off the beaten track. Can't be much of a lark."

Hillary smiled. "I've wondered that a few times myself. But I'll do a good job." She didn't want to go into any lengthy explanations of the circumstances that had brought her to Eagle's Watch.

"Hmm," the doctor said in a preoccupied way as he left her at the door. "You take good care of her now, you hear? And call me if you need me."

He was gone.

Hillary spent the next two hours working closely with Scotty in her room upstairs, finding her a mixture of eagerness and apprehension as her therapy began.

The young nurse began by gently massaging and manipulating her limbs and muscles. They still ached greatly from the soreness and stiffness that follows the aftermath of a stroke. Hillary was as careful as was humanly possible, and Scotty, for once, held her tongue and cooperated with the effort.

The passive exercises went well on that first attempt. Scotty had always been an active and alert woman, and her limbs moved relatively easily as

Hillary took her through the repetitious exercises. Up and down, up and down. She lifted each leg time after time, concentrating on the weaker right one and periodically halting to note her patient's pulse to make sure that the effort was not too much for her.

When it was time for Scotty to rest, Hillary lowered her comfortably into her bed so that she could be refreshed and ready to descend to the downstairs to take over her role as the owner of Eagle's Watch. She smiled down on the sleeping woman as she left the room, proud of the progress that had been made and even more excited about the future prospects of bringing Scotty back to her old, active form. So far so good.

* * *

Hillary wandered downstairs to check on the preparations for Scotty's lunch. She ran into Mitchell, drink in hand, and was introduced to the other newly arrived family members. Her first impression was an overwhelming one. Scotty had been disturbingly right in her analysis of her relatives and their intentions.

There was Arnold Weaver, a man whose age closely matched Scotty's, but who showed no resemblance to her in any other way. He was her first cousin, the closest relation, a self-indulgent little man always ready to sing his own praises, elegant from his well-manicured hands to his lavishly expensive clothing. He was as moody as he was vain, feeling the world owed him a living even though, according to Mitchell, he had never done a day's work in his life.

Next she met the Highfields, a portly, middle-aged couple sporting flashy clothes and talking excitedly in voices that were too loud for the room. Belinda Highfield was the daughter of a deceased cousin of Scotty's and went out of her way to appear concerned and caring about Priscilla.

But her eyes were shrewd and calculating, bringing to mind the cool stares of the family ancestors whose portraits hung on the staircase wall. The concern in her high-pitched voice just did not ring true.

Her thick-jowled husband, Franklin, had a puffy, weak-willed appearance, standing quietly in the overpowering shadow of his very vocal wife.

And Mitchell? How did she feel about him, seeing him among the others who had traveled to Eagle's Watch hoping to put themselves on the good side of the woman they thought might be close to death's door, hoping to get their share of the family estate. Vultures, Scotty had aptly called them.

But Mitchell, in his open and forthright manner, was humorous and direct in his approach to the whole situation, not trying to hide behind the see-through cloak of concern that the others attempted to delude the world with. Hillary respected him for his honesty, if not his motives.

When she made the announcement that Scotty was well enough to be joining the family for meals, that the doctor felt that she had every hope for a quick and relatively total recovery from her recent stroke, the reaction in the room was a strange one. The Highfields froze, drink in midair, the shock and disbelief etched on their unhappy faces. No doubt about their true emotions now. Scotty's recovery had been the last thing on their minds.

Arnold had been polite and discreet, making little comments into the stillness of the room. "Marvelous, marvelous. Really, the wonders of modern medicine!" But his comments were contradicted by the cold and disappointed look upon his face.

Only Mitchell's eyes were unreadable, un-laughing for once, but giving away no clue as to the feelings of their owner.

So this was Scotty's family. Hillary could see clearly the reasons that she had planned to hide herself away in the privacy of her room, rather than cope with this family full of undercurrents and questionable motives. They were people who had come in the name of concern, perhaps, but in reality, with very high hopes for their own personal gain.

Was Hillary right to have convinced Scotty to take part in these family meals? Would she be strong enough to go through with it?

But she had no time for further doubts, for at that moment the door to the dining room burst open to reveal the mistress of Eagle's Watch. She was confined to a wheelchair, perhaps, but she was wearing her best daytime finery, cheeks rosy with rouge and her head held high. Scotty was going through with it, all right, and with a lot of pride.

She waved away the hesitant Mr. Raymond who stood behind the chair, and with her stronger arm, pushed the button on the side of the motorized chair and crossed the room alone, to face the family that she had summed up so well.

Lunch was tense affair. Hillary sat, ever mindful of the spritely little woman who regally ruled from the head of the long table. Scotty ate her specially prepared menu with poise, if not with great dexterity. And she seemed oblivious (though Hillary knew instinctively that she was not) to the several pairs of eyes that continually surveyed her actions and judged her efforts.

The conversation was stilted and superficial, remarks made more to end the strained silence at the table than to communicate anything. Hillary was more than glad when the plates were cleared away, and the meal was over. Scotty had been amazingly quiet during the course of the meal, looking preoccupied and distant, though to Hillary's perceptive eye, she was constantly taking in all that was going on around her.

"It's so touching to have you all running to my bedside with your great concern," Scotty said finally, as the group was breaking up. Her voice dripped with the venomous sarcasm that she used so effectively. Hillary had to cough to cover the hint of a smile that was sneaking over her lips. Scotty could handle this bunch, she realized, and if Hillary was any judge, she was about to make that known.

"But really, as you can see, I'm fit as a fiddle at this point, and plan to be even fitter before much more time has passed. In other words, I have no intention of kicking the bucket yet."

The group stared at her in open-mouthed silence. She had their attention, that was certain.

"You are all welcome, of course, as members of the family, to stay on here at Eagle's Watch for as long as you may desire. Within reason," she added with a smirk, looking directly at her fancy but idle Cousin Arnold.

He intently picked at a piece of imaginary lint on the sleeve of his jacket.

"And now, the time has come for me to return to my suite to begin my afternoon therapy. Nurse Holt, as you know, is responsible for the progress I will be making. She is genuinely, refreshingly concerned about my well-being. A fact that will not go unnoticed, I assure you."

She turned to Hillary, and there was a devilish glint in her eye. Just what was Scotty up to? It wasn't long until the nurse found out.

"Hillary, perhaps you could contact Mr. Browning, my attorney in town, and ask him to stop by Eagle's Watch some time during the course of the week. I have a matter that I would like to discuss at length with him."

Belinda made an almost inaudible gasp at her words, her large mouth falling open as Scotty turned the motorized wheelchair and moved out of the room, the whirring sound almost deafening in the stillness of the room. Mr. Raymond appeared at the door to carry her upstairs.

Hillary stood frozen to the spot for a few minutes, wishing that she was out of range of the knifelike stares that were bombarding her from the four family members in the cold stone room. There was not much doubt as to the thoughts that were going on in their minds.

"She's finally going to make the will," whispered Belinda from between tightly clenched teeth. "That nurse..."

"Just what have you been saying to her, Hillary Holt, to coerce her so?" Arnold's face was white and strained. "This is just not fair."

Hillary just shook her head hopelessly. "You've got it all wrong. I don't know what this is all about." She turned and exited from the room, still feeling their eyes piercing into her back.

She darted up the steps, two at a time, anxious to place as much distance between herself and the very unfriendly faces below.

Scotty had meant her remarks to be sensational, to shake up these relatives that she was so annoyed with. To make them think that a will was in the making, that they had been overlooked suddenly for an unknown red-headed girl who had just arrived on the scene. She had shaken them up, all right.

But Scotty was just being dramatic. She had no intention of doing such a rash thing, in reality. She was playing with them, as Percival toyed with a mouse.

Hillary swallowed uncomfortably. A slight shiver ran up her spine. It didn't feel so very much like a game. She had seen the looks in the eyes of those people downstairs, and she had the overwhelmingly sinking sensation that it was she, and not they, who had been cast in the role of the mouse. And she didn't relish the thought one little bit.

Chapter 5

"Did you see the looks on their faces?" laughed Scotty. "I must say it really made my day."

Her clear eyes were sparkling with laughter, as Hillary took her through her leg motions in their afternoon session.

"I have to admit I didn't appreciate your little joke. You put me on quite a spot. They'll all hate me now. They're sure I'm a fortune hunter."

"Well, you're not, are you?"

"You know I'm not."

"Then I wouldn't worry about what they think. Call the lawyer, though, Hillary. I do intend to make up my will. I'm not getting any younger, as they say. No use tempting fate."

Hillary worked diligently, massaging the leg muscles in her patient's legs after their brief workout. "And just who are you going to leave the estate to, Scotty?"

"Nosy little thing, aren't you? All kidding aside, Hillary, I'm going to tell you, but I want you to promise me that you will never, ever tell anyone that you know."

"I promise."

"It's really very simple and unexciting. Besides healthy bequests to my servants and special friends, the bulk of the estate will be divided between Arnold, Mitchell, and the Highfields. They don't deserve it, of course, but they are family of a sort, and one has to consider these things. But I don't want them to know this. I rather enjoy seeing them squirm and try to outmaneuver each other. Just call it one of an old lady's few delights in life."

"Barbaric," said Hillary with a smile.

After all, it was Scotty's right to do as she pleased with her money, her right to confide or hold back her plans, as she saw best.

"Just do me a favor," Hillary said with a sigh. "Can you keep me out of this?" She remembered the accusing glances that had followed her across the dining room. She would have to come into daily contact with those people, and she didn't relish the thought.

"I'm sorry, Hillary. I guess I did rather put you in a bad position. Can we chalk it up to a blind impulse? A whim of a senile old woman?"

She gave Hillary a dramatic, appealing look.

"The only thing senile about you is your warped sense of humor," countered Hillary. She measured and charted Scotty's vital signs and settled her under the fluffy comforters on her bed. "Time to rest now. I'm going downstairs to attempt to soothe the troubled waters you've stirred up for me with your relatives."

Scotty studied her for a moment. "Well, if anyone can, you can, my dear. I dare say you'll have Mitchell Morrison jumping through a hoop in no time at all, for starters."

Hillary felt a blush rising in her freckled cheeks.

"Really, Scotty, I don't think he and I have much in common."

The old woman's laugh rang out in the room. "I can see Matilda was very right about you. Too much burying one's head in one's books can leave you missing a lot of the fun in life. Give yourself a chance to play and enjoy life, Hillary. You're only young once."

The nurse had a very unsettling lump in the back of her throat as she headed for the stairs. She was shocked that her far-off aunt had known her habits so well to form such an opinion, and equally shocked to realize that there was more than a grain of truth in her insight.

A very pensive Hillary traveled down the long stairway, for once without giving even a glance to the sober portraits she passed along the way.

As her toes barely touched the bottom step of the castle stairway, she was startled by the sudden appearance of Arnold Weaver, his elderly face wearing a cool mask of concern and friendliness, so strikingly different from the accusing stare it had worn only a few short hours before.

"Well, what a coincidence to run into you like this, Nurse Holt. I was just thinking of you."

She regarded his face, its catlike eyes searching hers evenly and deeply. But she doubled that there had been a bit of coincidence in his arrival in the foyer at the same instant as hers. Indeed, his well-timed appearance and easy remarks sounded staged to Hillary's ears, as if he had been eagerly waiting in the wings for his cue to make them.

He moved very lithely and was amazingly light on his feet for his advanced years. Her mind kept automatically comparing him to a cat: his movements, his narrowed eyes, his low, self-satisfied voice that flowed from deep in his throat like a teasing purr. He was a very difficult man to trust.

"And how is dear Priscilla this afternoon? I must say, she looked well and fit at luncheon." His tone was friendly, concerned. It made Hillary very nervous.

"She is doing amazingly well. Mr. Weaver. We have quite high hopes and expectations for her."

"Have you now?" His face was still smiling, but his eyes were not. "And have you contacted the lawyer that she requested to see? I can't help but wonder if that would be a good idea. After all, handling burdensome legal details might be too much of a strain on her, don't you agree?"

"It is her wish. I can't see that a simple consultation would pose any difficulties."

"Yes. I see. And has she perhaps mentioned to you the business that she wishes to discuss? Perhaps I could be of some service to her, instead of bringing the attorney all the way to Eagle's Watch for some mere trifle."

It was very apparent that he did not want Priscilla to see the lawyer, that he was more than slightly concerned about the business to be transacted, the fact that a will might be in the offing.

And why would that bother him? Quite obviously he had much doubt that the will would benefit him. And if Scotty were to die without having a will, Arnold Weaver, as her next of kin, would legally have a right to the entire inheritance. And there was no doubt that that very thought was sitting heavily upon his mind.

Hillary looked at his well-lined face, its facade of charm and concern clashing wildly with the thoughts she knew must be going on in his self-centered mind. She wanted no quarrels, no upsets with him, but she was finding him to be increasingly distasteful to her. She wanted to get away from him and his false words.

"I'm sure the attorney will be more than willing to make the trip, Mr. Weaver. Miss Scott must be a very important client to him. I don't think you need to worry about the strain that such procedures may cause. With my care, and the doctor's supervision, I can assure you that she will be in no medical difficulty. Excuse me now. I was just on my way out."

Her words were clipped and short. Her intention in coming downstairs had been to patch up the misunderstandings that had set her off so poorly with the rest of the guests in the house, but standing in the gloomy foyer, listening to the smooth words spoken by the suave little freeloader who stood in front of her, she felt her task was hopeless.

She had a sudden and overwhelming urge to rush out into the bright fresh air outside the thick front door. She left Arnold Weaver with a shallow smile and moved quickly across the stone floor of the foyer, pulling open the heavy black door, and plummeting forth into the warmth and sunlight of the afternoon.

And Arnold Weaver stood at the bottom of the long stairway watching her exit, his face for once stripped of the usually well-controlled charm and good-natured appearance that he tried to wear. If Hillary had been able to read the accusing and hateful thoughts that filled his white-haired head, his growing fear that she was quickly and fully becoming an important person in the life of his unpredictable Cousin Priscilla, if she had been able to see the selfish and penetrating stare of his squinted eyes as he watched her depart, she would have felt much less exalted by the glorious day that surrounded her.

She made a very pretty picture as she walked slowly in the afternoon heat, her white uniform crisp and bright, her red hair shiny and bouncing as the sun picked up its sparkling highlights. She walked around to the back of the castle, following a small gravel path that hugged the castle wall. The sound of the ocean below echoed constantly with its pounding waves.

She walked to the edge of the rocky expanse that provided the foundation for Eagle's Watch, raising her eyes to gaze out to the never-ending blueness that was the Atlantic Ocean. Far in the distance, she could see a sailing vessel, a mere speck on the horizon.

Only yesterday, she had stood in almost this same spot, seeing the view from the castle cliff for the first time. She had been resentful, nervous, unsure about her arrival, and the scene had seemed dismal and overpowering. Now, she found herself viewing the same scene with a breathless feeling of wonder, of respect, of beauty. It was a lonely spot, to be sure, but in that loneliness it possessed an incomparable aura of peace.

She sat down on a nearby rock and enjoyed the heat of the sun's rays beating against her back. The air felt clear and healthful, despite the heat, and the pungent aroma of salty ocean drifted to her waiting nostrils.

It was a beautiful area, this secluded part of Maine. Too deserted for her to want to remain forever, but it certainly had a special charm. Suddenly she realized that she was very glad to be there, to be away from the pressures and responsibility that had been her life.

Scotty was right. One had to open one's mind up in order to live and enjoy life, to be willing to risk experiencing new things, to grow.

There was a bond growing between her and Scotty, she knew, and the realization of that brought a warm feeling into her heart. Hillary had felt that she had been alone in the world for a long time.

But Scotty had said that Miss Matilda had followed her progress every step of the way. Someone had cared.

She heaved a great sigh and watched a single bird fly overhead.

Hillary would try to take Scotty's advice, to look at her from all angles, to live. And someday she would return to the surgical nursing that she loved. Also, she firmly promised herself, she would meet her Aunt Matilda, no matter what the complications, to thank her for everything.

Feeling refreshed, she returned to the castle and its challenges.

Chapter 6

In her newly found mood of peace, Hillary decided to wander around the castle for a short while to see it in the daylight hours when the bright rays of sunlight filtered in through the thick glass windows.

She was drawn to the kitchen area, where she found dinner preparations were well underway. The room buzzed with the steady bustle of activity. Mrs. Raymond was in her usual scurry, darting around the counters and appliances, giving orders to her small staff.

"Please, Annie, not too much salt in the soup. Mr. Mitchell definitely doesn't care for too much salt."

"He'll eat what he gets, like everybody else around here," came the gruff voice of the gray-haired cook who stood leaning over the steaming pots on the stove. She was tall and massive-looking in her white uniform, her more than ample figure almost bursting through the seams. "I'll cater to Mr. Mitchell when he pays my salary, and not before. If you ask me, you pay too much attention to that young dandy."

"Nonsense, Annie. A young man like that needs someone to fuss over him." Mrs. Raymond's usually stern face looked vulnerable for once, but the look passed quickly. "Daisy," she called, "where are you?"

A trim little blonde in a well-starched uniform appeared at the pantry door. Her saucer like eyes regarded the housekeeper for a moment, then lit on Hillary, still standing unnoticed in the hallway door.

"We've got company, Mrs. Raymond."

The housekeeper turned on her heel to meet Hillary.

"Why. Nurse Holt, what can we do for you?"

"This is just a social visit. I thought I'd like to meet the rest of the staff."

And so the introductions were made. Annie had been cooking for Miss Scott for so many years that she had lost count. Daisy, the young attractive maid, had arrived only that very morning, to help deal with the guests. She seemed remarkably quiet and withdrawn, but Hillary hoped that with time, she and this other new arrival might become friends. It was a heartening feeling to know that there was another young woman in the household, one that she might have something in common with.

She left the kitchen a few moment's later and made her call to the Scott family lawyer from the phone in the downstairs study. She was told that Mr. Browning was out of town for the week. He would not be able to come to Eagle's Watch to consult with Priscilla Scott until he returned. Scotty's will would have to wait.

Hillary browsed through the shelves of books that lined the sunless study after she replaced the receiver in its cradle. She selected an elegant leather-bound volume of poetry to read after she retired to her room at night. As she turned to leave the study, she found Mitchell standing in the broad doorway, leaning rakishly against the carved molding, looking handsome and boyish in his well-fitting suit.

"Don't tell me our nurse is an intellectual, as well as an explorer," he said gaily, referring to her evening expedition through the echoing castle. "What are you reading?"

"Poetry. I like to read it to relax at night."

"I would think a girl like you would have other plans for relaxing at night."

His teasing eyes were dancing suggestively as he crossed the room toward her, and she felt her face getting blushingly hot.

"Yes, I also enjoy sorting pill bottles and reading medical charts," she teased back. "And once in a while, I sit down and organize my medical kit. There's no end to my exciting talents."

He threw his head back and laughed wholeheartedly. "If you've got some time before you return to the medical battlefield upstairs, how about taking a little walk with me outside? It's a beautiful day."

She thought of the exhilarating sunlight outdoors. She thought of taking a walk with Mitchell. Both ideas were pleasant ones. To return to the fresh air would be a delight, to share some time with this personable young man, Scotty's youngest relative, would be intriguing.

She smiled at his expectant face and agreed to take a jaunt outdoors for a short time while Scotty still slept. The delighted look on his face at her acceptance made her feel lighthearted and gay. She might have little in common with Mitchell Morrison, but there was certainly something to Scotty's suggestion that she let go and enjoy life a bit!

And so Hillary left the darkness of the castle for the second time that day, and returned to the rocky path that hovered above the ocean, this time with the happy-go-lucky Mitchell at her side.

They sat on the high rocks that had quickly become Hillary's favorite thinking place, and the minutes ticked by in the sunny afternoon as she learned about the young man beside her.

He lived alone in a small apartment in New York City and made his living by "buying and selling" anything he could get his hands on. He ran his own rather unorthodox business, handling an assortment of items, from antiques, furniture, and jewelry, to real estate. He called himself a "jack of all trades" in the selling market, not even trying to hide the pride and confidence he felt in his work.

"It sounds as though you do pretty well for yourself," Hillary commented after a while. She watched him anxiously to see his reaction, wanting to hear him disavow any need for his great-aunt's inheritance.

But typical of Mitchell, he threw his head back and laughed with fervor. "Hillary, I swear I can see right through you. I'm sorry, my dear, but I won't say that I am not in need of Aunt Priscilla's money. And if I did say such a thing, it would be blatantly naive of you to believe me. Truthfully, I would sorely love to have a say in what will happen to this place after she has gone. I would adore the freedom it would give me.

"However," he said, and his rakish grin returned, "it is easy to see that the issue is not an important one at the moment. She's in better health than the rest of us put together, and as an adorably good sport, I truly hope that she stays that way. So, now I've made my confession. Do you think less of me?"

He reached out and took her hand and smiled brightly into her green eyes. He made her feel very funny inside. After all, at least he was honest about his intentions. And you really couldn't blame anyone for wishing that an inheritance would come his way. Or could you?

"Now, take that old Uncle Arnold, for instance. I swear, he'd sell us all to the gypsies to get his hands on the money. And that's no exaggeration. He has always complained that he had a right to some of it anyway, that his mother, who was Priscilla's aunt, had been wrongly disinherited for eloping with an unsuitable scoundrel way back in the dark ages. Perhaps it was unfair, but it's all water under the bridge now. That man hasn't done a day's work in his entire life, and spends the greater part of his time traveling from one estate to the next, portable house guest to any gentry who will have him, and are stupid enough to put up with him.

"At least you can't put me in that category, Hillary. I do work for a living!"

She laughed at his mocking self-defense. "And what about the Highfields?"

"Oh, they are a pair, I'll tell you. He has a little bad habit that keeps cropping up and setting them back a bit. It's called gambling. I must say, he's about the worst that I've ever seen. He can't resist a bet, no matter what the odds.

"If you bet him that the sun would go down this evening, he'd bet money that it wouldn't. They spend the better part of their days trying to clear up all the bets and bad debts. He works for some big corporation in Buffalo, but never makes enough to keep his little lady in the manner to which she'd like to be accustomed. He's a rather inoffensive little fellow. I feel rather sorry for him. But she's a tough old bird."

"You don't sound like you have too much affection for your relatives."

"Affection. That's a new word in our family vocabulary. We can't stand each other, and Aunt Priscilla can't stand any of us either. But we keep coming back for more, still hoping to be the one she dislikes the least, the one who'll end up with the prize when the time comes. We always figured it would have to be one of us. After all, who else?"

He paused, and his dark eyes were suddenly looking deeply into Hillary's. "And how about you,

Hillary Holt? Why are you here? Was there any truth to the bomb of a rumor that Aunt Priscilla alluded to at lunch today? Are you destined to be the new heiress of Eagle's Watch?"

Her mouth hung open in wonder. What should she say? She wished with all of her heart that she could tell him the things that Scotty had planned, to clear her name and show that she had nothing to do with the inner goings-on in this unpredictable family. But she had given Scotty her promise. She could not speak of her patient's plans. But she could defend herself.

"I have no intention of any such thing." Her eyes were too bright, she knew, her cheeks were burning.

"Now don't get huffy, Hillary. I just couldn't help wondering what a girl like you was doing in this godforsaken place, why on earth you had buried yourself up here when the whole world is out there waiting to be enjoyed. I didn't want to offend you. Personally, I couldn't care less if you did have ulterior motives in coming to Eagle's Watch. People do what they have to do, that's my motto in life. Though I must say that my nose will be out of joint if you manage to accomplish in a few days' time, what we've been trying to do for years and years!"

Her face was a blaze of color.

"My dear, you certainly are striking when you're mad. I'll have to make you mad more often."

He patted her hand and smiled his teasing smile, and calmed some of the anger that had welled up inside her. He was a paradox, this handsome young man. He had a way of disarming her, away of catching her off guard. You do what you have to do, he had said. And that was the way that he lived his life. He would not have been even slightly surprised if she had grand notions of being the mistress of Eagle's Watch. He would not have judged her harshly, any more than he judged his own motives. Mitchell was certainly different from anyone she had ever known before. They walked back along the rocky path to the castle, now quiet, their footsteps muffled by the constant beat of the ocean's waves.

The rest of the day passed quickly. Hillary held another short therapy session with Scotty and found herself continually impressed with the diligence and remarkable determination of her patient as she was guided through the paces of her exercise routine.

Dinner was an affair that left the young nurse with mixed emotions. Once again, Scotty ruled at the head of the table, dressed elegantly in a striking dress of deep purple, as regal as it was old-fashioned. Around her withered neck, she wore a valuable gold and pearl pendant, its antique setting catching everyone's eye in the flickering candlelight. Many pairs of eyes assessed it eagerly, a fact which Hillary found disconcerting. But Scotty, true to form, was enjoying her relatives' not-too-subtle appraisal of the heirloom.

Scotty refrained from making any additional comments about her intention to make a will, which made Hillary more at ease, though she was still conscious of the sidelong glances and resentful looks that occasionally came her way, evidence that at least some of the family members still regarded her in the same accusing light that they had at the noon meal.

But the dinner was delicious, and superbly served, as Daisy moved gracefully and easily around the long table with the courses, under the constant scrutinizing eye of Mrs. Raymond. When the food was consumed, and the places cleared away, the group rapidly dispersed, a sign that they were several individuals temporarily housed under one roof but whose lives were distinctly separate. No one had as yet made any mention of his intention to leave Eagles' Watch in the near future.

Hillary settled Scotty for the night, and found that she was tired from the day's activities and emotions. Curling up with her book of poetry, she relaxed in her cozy room, drifting off into a restful sleep as the nighttime breeze gently ruffled the curtains at her window.

Chapter 7

"I swear, Hillary, if the good Lord had intended my arms and legs to move into the positions that you are attempting to put them into, he would have made them out of rubber, instead of flesh and blood."

Scotty grouched good-naturedly at Hillary a few days later, making a big noise about the repetitious and sometimes strenuous routines that she went through. But she complied all the same, her eyes still smiling and hopeful and willing, despite the sarcasm and teasing criticism in her voice.

"If the good Lord had intended you to sit in a chair for the rest of your days, Scotty, he would have stilled your mouth, too, so that we who have to be around you would be able to find life more bearable. As it is, we'll have to push you, rubber legs and all, and get you back on your feet for our own self-defense." Hillary finished up the exercise and rubbed some soothing lotion on the tired leg muscles. They had grown less tender already, as the circulation improved and the strength began to return.

"They certainly do make nurses bossy these days."

Two pairs of bright eyes met in the morning sunlight, one pair old and one pair young, but both laughing and sparkling, as patient and nurse regarded each other with affection. The day had begun well.

A few moments later, the door to the bedroom echoed with a resounding knock, and Hillary opened it to find Dr. Newburg, black bag in hand, in a suit not much less rumpled than the one he'd worn on their first meeting.

"Good morning, Doctor. I wasn't at all sure that we would see you today. Come in, come in."

"I thought I'd check, Nurse Holt, to make sure that Priscilla hadn't thrown you to the lions. Nurses are hard to come by these days."

The gray-haired man passed her in the doorway smiling in a friendly way to Scotty across the room, as if amused by her haughty pose. She sat regally in her wheelchair and looked out upon him like a queen surveying her humble subject.

"To be sure, I am faring extremely well under Nurse Holt's excellent care. Much better than under yours, if I may say so."

Dr. Newburg's face broke into a wrinkled smile and he gave a deep chuckle. His years of experience with Priscilla Scott had taught him to respect and appreciate her sharp tongue and mind alike.

"Well, I'm sorry you're not delighted with my medical prowess, Priscilla. I've brought along someone who will be helping me out for a while, and maybe he will be more your cup of tea. Priscilla

Scott, meet Dr. Kent Harris, only son of my late best friend, Dr. Marcus Harris."

After opening the door to let Dr. Newburg enter, Hillary had turned her back to the hallway.

Now, she suddenly turned, embarrassed to have missed seeing the unknown man who must have been standing directly behind her, ignored and unnoticed.

"I'm so sorry," she began, trying to cover up for her oversight, and trying to welcome him into the room. "I really didn't see you there..."

Her words melted away on her lips as her eyes focused on the tall, broad-framed figure that now stood directly in the doorway.

"Dr. Harris, let me introduce Miss Hillary Holt, who may look as slight and delicate as a gentle ocean breeze but who has the nerves and determination of a gale, to have dared to take on my favorite patient here at Eagle's Watch. And succeeding famously, I might add."

I he young doctor extended his hand quietly and Hillary took it, gazing up into his dark eyes. Her eyes felt glued to his, hypnotized, and she felt a kind of solid strength emanating from him, an instant bond of interest and rapport.

But almost as soon as the feeling had passed between them, a kind of dark shadow seemed to come down over those expressive eyes of his, as if the magical feeling that she had experienced had been a glimpse into his inner self, exposed when he had been caught off guard. But whatever it had been, it was gone. His voice, deep and full as she had expected it to be, was merely courteous and professional.

"I'm certainly glad to meet you, Miss Scott. This is quite a place you have here." He turned to Hillary. "And Nurse Holt. I'm sure that we will work well together. Doctor, shall we make our examination? There are still a number of calls for us to make this morning."

"Of course, of course," bustled Dr. Newburg. He began his examination of Priscilla's progress, testing the muscles for their returning strength, noticing the decreasing soreness and stiffness, checking the carefully plotted vital signs in the medical report. Dr. Harris watched each step of the way, as Hillary assisted the aging doctor with automatic motions. She could almost feel the presence of the young doctor behind her, a tingling, electrical sensation that made her stomach feel flighty and her knees weak. What on earth was happening to her?

"Well," said Dr. Newburg as he completed his examination, "I'm quite impressed. You two are making quite an unbeatable team." He shut his black bag with a snap. "And now, we'd best be moving on, as Dr. Harris suggests. The young certainly know how to make progress, eh, Priscilla?"

And after a few parting comments and a promise to return on Friday, the two doctors disappeared into the hallway and were gone.

Hillary tried to overcome the slightly breathless feeling that remained with her, tucking

Scotty in for her nap, avoiding the old woman's eyes that kept looking into hers with a knowing glance.

But the nurse wasn't ready to talk about this feeling yet, and Scotty had the sensitivity to realize it. All Hillary wanted to do was to retire to her room and think quietly about the young man that she had just met, the handsome young doctor who had said no more than a few polite words to her, but who, in a brief flash of time, had touched her heart and had cast a spell over her.

The next few days passed more slowly than Hillary ever would have imagined. Her sessions with Scotty went well, each morning and afternoon they went through the now well-known routines faithfully and determinedly. The small motor coordination skills were a challenge at first. Scotty would hold a small rubber ball in the palm of her hand and attempt to squeeze the not-too-adept fingers of her right hand around it, the muscles still taut and difficult to stretch.

Her left hand had not been affected greatly in the overall stroke damage, and she used it constantly to help herself manipulate the weaker limb.

She progressed, with much effort and much diligence, a determined look etched upon her aged face. Hillary was very proud of her.

Mealtimes were the only times that either of them came into contact with the other family members, who were still the comfortable guests of Eagle's Watch. Mitchell, with his boyishly crooked grin and dancing eyes, had cornered Hillary on a few occasions to accompany her on an outside excursion around the grounds of the castle, but each time, she begged off, giving the excuse of fatigue.

But fatigue was, truthfully, the last thing that she was suffering from. Instead, her mind and her body seemed to be running at a ferocious pace, and in the stillness of Eagle's Watch, with the sound of the waves the only company as she daydreamed in her room, she found herself continually thinking of that broad frame in the doorway, the person to whom she had been so instantly drawn. Dr. Kent Harris.

She knew so little about him, which didn't seem to matter at all. She kept remembering the deep resonance of his voice, his neatly cut dark hair, his dark eyes that had told her so much before his defenses had gone up.

And why had he gotten defensive? To shutter those windows to his soul out of fear that she might see too much? All she knew was that she had looked into those eyes, and had been gripped by a force that she had never known before. The barest reminder of it made her feel lighthearted and dizzy.

It was so different from the carefree, laughing way she felt when she was with Mitchell, so different from anything she had ever experienced.

Her mind wandered as she counted the slow hours until the arrival of Friday. She hoped she would find out more about Dr. Kent Harris. Would she feel the same way when she saw him again?

Would she, in fact, see him again? And was she possibly exaggerating her feelings for him? Were they imaginary?

She was totally unaware of Scotty's amused and thoughtful eyes, taking in her dilemma with the insight and wisdom of one who understands, one who cares, of one who knows the pain and the joy that life can bring.

Chapter 8

Friday finally arrived. Hillary awakened with an expectant feeling, long before the small alarm on the table next to her bed gave off its insistent clamor. She bathed and dressed without hesitation, eagerly anticipating the doctor's visit, and hoping earnestly that his newfound associate would be at his side.

For the first time since her arrival at Eagle's Watch, the morning arrived without a hint of sunshine. The sky outside her high window loomed gray and dark, the ocean had a purplish, perilous look to it. A light misting of rain was falling in the cooler air, the dampness of the day was permeating the thick walls of the stone castle and casting a chill over the rooms.

It was far from a pleasant day, but Hillary faced it with a cheery heart. She ate her breakfast quickly, trying to chat in a friendly way with Daisy when she arrived with the tray, to open the door to companionship with the young blonde to whom she was so close in age. But Daisy insistently kept her eyes lowered in a subservient way and failed to respond with anything more than a polite answer to her friendly questions.

She arrived at Scotty's room earlier than she usually did, but found her patient awake and lively and in a good humor.

"I simply love this weather, Hillary. It reminds me of London, you know. Makes me feel young again."

With Hillary's deft help, she was soon dressed and in her chair.

"I can feel myself getting stronger each day," Scotty squealed delightedly, as she moved her right foot slowly without assistance. "See that? I'll be up and dancing before you know it. Now let's get these exercises going with vim and dispatch!" Her eyes were twinkling. "The doctor comes this morning, and it might just be a good chance for us to acquaint ourselves with this new associate of his. Is that agreeable to you, Hillary, my dear?"

She took her daily medication and looked at Hillary with wide and innocent eyes.

"Don't think you have a corner on the market, Nurse Holt. Remember, I was young once, too, as hard as that may be to believe!"

Hillary smiled. "And what did you think of Dr. Harris? Do you blame me for thinking about him?"

"Certainly not. Even with his rather brisk manner the other day, he exuded a certain masculine charm. Very impressive. Though I think that there is something weighing heavily on his mind. He's under stress, I think, and he's trying to cope."

Hillary thought over Scotty's perceptive words. They completed the exercise routine in record time.

During a rest time, Hillary brought up the subject of the artist's studio in the first tower room, sure that Scotty had been the creator of the sculptures that she had admired on her evening tour of the castle.

Hillary's heart gave a lurch as she saw Scotty's eyes fill up with tears. "Yes, that is my studio. Was my studio, in the past tense. It is a part of my life that I miss desperately." The room was very still.

"It may well be a part of your life again, you know, if you keep working with the dedication that you have been showing."

"Don't pacify me, Hillary." Scotty looked down at her hands in her lap, blue veined and slow. "I can't even imagine these hands reacting as they used to."

"We've just begun. You've got to be patient. Perhaps if we brought some clay down, you could work it in your hands as a part of your therapy. We could fix up a spot here for you to work."

"No." The word was emphatic and it was final. "I cannot work with clay while I'm confined to this chair. I cannot work with clay with my hands gnarled and useless. When the day comes that I can climb those stone steps, return to my studio, and create with two able hands, then we will talk about it. I am an artist, Hillary. I have pride in my work. To do less than the best would be an insult."

Hillary nodded soundlessly, realizing the depth of feeling that lay behind Scotty's words. She would not bring it up again until the time was right. They began Scotty's hand-therapy routine with the rubber ball.

Today, Scotty handled the ball with such intensity that Hillary called a halt early, to check her vital signs, worried about the tiny beads of perspiration that had appeared on her patient's brow. Her pulse was slightly elevated, a sign that her emotional outburst coupled with the physical exercise had been over-exciting and dangerous.

Hillary helped her to her bed to rest and await the doctor's arrival.

The two doctors arrived in a short time, and Hillary reported the progress Scotty had been making, along with her recent upset and its consequence to her pulse. A check in her resting condition showed the pulse had returned to normal, which was a relief. But it clearly pointed out to Hillary the danger of over-excitement and overexertion, and she vowed to keep things on a more even keel in the future.

Concerned about Scotty's condition, she had consulted with the doctor conscientiously, her thoughts momentarily distracted from the young quiet doctor who sat in the corner of the room, silently going over the patient's chart. But when her duties were done, when her patient was safe and relaxed, Hillary's strange awareness of Kent Harris's presence began to hover over her once again.

How she wished that she were more outgoing and gregarious, ready to glide across the room and sit herself down by his side, striking up an easy conversation. But her feet felt like lead, and she couldn't approach him. Deep in the file, he seemed to take no notice of her whatsoever.

Dr. Newburg finished his conversation with Scotty and repacked his black bag, shutting it with a snap. Dr. Harris rose, prepared to move on to their next scheduled call.

Hillary felt her heart begin to sink. She had awaited this morning for several days, and had found herself still strongly attracted to Kent Harris. The feeling had not just been in her imagination. But she had had no chance to speak to him, and he had not attempted to speak to her.

Scotty came to the rescue.

"Dr. Newburg, I was wondering if you and your associate, Dr. Harris, would join us for Sunday dinner this week. Some of the members of my family are in town and staying with us, and we'd love to have you join us."

Dr. Newburg laughed. "Your family I can do without, Priscilla, to tell the truth, and so can you! But, yes, I'd be delighted to come and share in your company, and especially to get some of Annie's scrumptious cooking. It's the best in New England, you know. How about you, Dr. Harris? A man living alone could do with a home-cooked meal."

"Certainly. Thank you very much. Miss Scott. I'd be delighted." His voice was polite and noncommittal, but at least he was coming. As the two left the room, Kent glanced at Hillary, his face wearing the faintest trace of a pleased smile.

Hillary's heart was singing. She would have another chance to see him, to be close to him, to learn more about him. Was he under stress, as Scotty had suggested? Was he unhappy? Mourning? Had he been hurt in a way that made him defensive and shy? She remembered the way their eyes had met the first time she had seen him. How she longed to see that look again!

She tucked Scotty in for a late morning nap, and then headed for her room, her feet soundless and dancing on the hallway floor, her voice humming a happy tune under her breath.

She opened the door to her room and gasped in surprise. For someone had entered it in her absence during the course of the morning, someone who would not have wanted to be seen.

Scrawled in lipstick across the massive mirror that was hung over her dressing table was the word LEAVE.

It shouted out to her in its simplicity, its maliciousness. Who could have written it? And why? Perhaps it was a harmless prank, and its instigator would soon appear at the door and expose his or her rather macabre sense of humor. But perhaps it was not.

Curled up, sound asleep in the chair in the corner of the room, she found Percival, Scotty's powerful black cat. Following on the heels of the intruder, he must have been left in the room. He stretched and yawned lazily, regarding her with large marblelike eyes, eyes that knew the identity of her unwanted visitor. How simple things would be if that cat could talk!

Chapter 9

No one appeared at the door to own up to the rather dramatic defacement of Hillary's mirror, however, and she found herself standing in the middle of her spacious room for several minutes, in a quandary about what to do next.

Who on earth would have done such a thing? It seemed almost childish, silly. And yet, there was no denying that the red splotches that screamed out from across the glass made her feel fearful, uncomfortable.

She retrieved a cloth from the nearby bath, and set about removing the traces of the misused lipstick.

Should she make a scene, call attention to the action, and demand to know who was involved? The thought was not a pleasant one. She was already far from a popular figure in the echoing castle, and to falsely accuse one or another of the inhabitants would make her position even worse, to be sure. And such an action would probably not even bring the results that she wished, since the culprit was not likely to own up to his deeds in such a spot.

And Scotty? Hillary remembered the way her pulse had climbed in the morning hours, stimulated by the emotional upset. How her temper would flare to hear about this. The young nurse pushed away any intention of bringing her experience out into the open. The threat it would bring to Scotty's health was not worth the relief that she would feel if she uncovered the person who had stolen into her room.

The dreary day moved on. Hillary followed her now-familiar schedule, but her mind kept returning to the startling sight of the brash word on her mirror, the word that had long since been removed from the glass, but was now etched indelibly in her memory.

* * *

"I do hope you are going to wear something other than a uniform tonight," said Scotty teasingly, as Sunday afternoon was drawing to a close. The weekend had passed fairly quickly for Hillary, and the time for the awaited dinner party that would include Dr. Newburg and Dr. Harris was near at hand. Hillary was assisting Scotty into a flowing blue gown, its folds settling over her slim body with a graceful elegance as she sat upright in her chair. Even at eighty-four, hindered by the effects of her stroke, she was a handsome woman, full of poise, full of style. She added a diamond choker to her long neck and clipped on an accompanying set of earrings.

"Did you bring a dress, or some other such creation, Hillary? It really does no harm to look one's best when you are trying to attract someone's attention."

The girl felt embarrassed. "But I am just a nurse here."

"Don't give me such a lot of bunk, Hillary Holt. We can be honest with each other, don't you think? It's easy to see that you think that young doctor is something else, which I wholeheartedly agree about. But it's also obvious that he's a man with other matters burdening his mind. So if you want to make any kind of impression, you may need to make a little extra effort. Now, do you have a dress or not?"

Hillary smiled sheepishly. She thought of the floor-length pale green dress that she had so impulsively bought after her nursing-school graduation, a dress that had hung unworn in her closet since the day she had first unwrapped it. She nodded.

"I'm not much good at these things. Scotty. I'll probably mess things up royally."

"Hogwash, girl! Just be yourself. There's nothing more to succeeding in life than that." The old woman shook her head. "It's about time you came to grips with things like this. Hillary. Life passes more quickly than we can ever imagine." She patted Hillary's hand fondly. "Now get out of here, and go and get ready for the evening ahead. It's not often that we have welcome visitors here at Eagle's Watch, and I intend to enjoy every fleeting second of it."

Her stronger hand shooed Hillary to the door. "Don't come back until you've changed from Hillary the Nurse to Hillary the Beautiful Girl. This is a party, not a medical convention."

Her smile gave Hillary the confidence she needed. Hillary descended the long staircase a short time later, after Scotty had been carried down in Mr. Raymond's strong arms. She was delightedly surprised at the feeling of exhilaration that had risen up from deep within her, as she had so eagerly dressed for the evening ahead.

In the soft glow of the huge stone foyer, the picture she made was a breathtaking one. Her dress was airy and light, skimming the floor with fold after fold of soft green chiffon, her bodice fitted and cut exquisitely to show off her delicate neck and shoulders. She wore no jewelry at all, except for a thin gold chain that hugged her neck, but the green shade of the dress made the green of her eyes explode with a light of their own, like two priceless emeralds. She was full of the excitement of anticipation, and it set her complexion to glowing.

The doctors had already arrived when she entered the dining room; Scotty had been placed in her chair. A sudden hush settled over the room full of people—the family members and guests and servants.

In a flash, Hillary noticed Mitchell's delighted eye, the Highfields' reaction of surprise, the shifty look of appraisal from Arnold Weaver. But she paid little attention to them, beyond that first impression, because her eyes were totally drawn to the face of Kent Harris.

And his look was worth a million words. For a moment, the dark clouds that seemed to hover over his dark head gently disappeared, and his face lit up with awe and delight. It was a heartfelt look of approval and interest that swept over him as if by reflex.

But the clouds did not remain away for long. For no sooner had she taken a few more steps into the room than the shadows fell over his face once more. The preoccupied, unhappy look that armored him fell back into place.

But Hillary's heart was alive with hope. Her blood was singing in her veins. He *had* noticed her. He had been far from oblivious to her presence. She could not have mistaken the look in his eyes.

He was a man with a burden to bear, a burden that made him unresponsive to the world around him, made him seek the safety and solace of his own private thoughts.

But perhaps the day would come when she would be able to be a part of those thoughts, too, to understand whatever trial must be borne, to once again see the glowing light that she had just witnessed momentarily on his face, and to kindle that flame so that it need not be extinguished so quickly.

She surprised herself with the depth of her emotion, with this unexplained feeling for the quiet giant of a doctor who had so recently crossed her path.

But then, since the arrival of her Aunt Matilda's note bidding her to appear in this out-of-the-way place, her life had been full of new thoughts, new feelings, new emotions.

The dinner went splendidly. The room, often cold and dark in the daylight hours with its windows sheltered from the bright rays of the sun, looked magnificent tonight, bathed in an abundance of candlelight and elegance. The chandelier that was suspended dramatically from the high ceiling was aglow for the first time since Hillary had arrived. The fire in the oversized fireplace made the room feel cozier and more homelike than she would ever have believed possible.

Its heat took some of the dampness away and cast a reassuring warmth in the air. Though the summer days were hot in northern Maine, the nights could be cold. And in the deep interior of Eagle's Watch, the nighttime chill often was more appropriate for November than for July.

The family was on their best behavior during the delicious meal that Mrs. Raymond and Daisy served at the well-set table. Dr. Newburg was right in his appraisal of Annie's cooking talents. Each mouthful was even more satisfying than the last.

The champagne was chilled, the service was smooth, and the conversation was light and enjoyable. An outsider regarding the group that sat around the spacious table would have been surprised to learn of the undercurrents and resentments that were simmering beneath the facade of the jovial party atmosphere.

And how Scotty enjoyed herself! She took great pride in showing off her hard-earned improvement in her ability to manipulate her eating utensils. And she made wry little jokes about waiting for the day when she would graduate from eating "mush" to normal food. She sat poised and proud at the head of her table, gracious to her guests and even to her family.

By the end of the meal, Hillary felt a little lightheaded because of the wine, which she was not used to drinking.

As the table was cleared away, the family and guests proceeded to leave the dining room to socialize and partake of their coffee and dessert. Scotty showed signs of tiring, and so Hillary called for Mr. Raymond to carry her back up the wide stairway to her room, following them up the steps to help her patient prepare for the night.

It was only a few moments later when she descended the steps, silently and very carefully, for her head was still not as clear as usual. She stood for a minute in the broad expanse of foyer that separated the two wings of the house, straining her ears to hear in which direction the guests had settled. She heard more than she had bargained for.

From the flow of sound, the whole group was evidently seated in the living room, to the left of where she stood. Mrs. Highfield's voice sang out above the rest in its haughty, ear-piercing pitch, and her words came clearly through.

"And so, Dr. Newburg, we merely thought that we had better confide in you, for Priscilla's sake, of course. After all, we know practically nothing at all about that nurse. She appeared here out of nowhere and has gone her merry way ingratiating herself with my aunt, poor condition that she is in. I've heard of cases like this before, of girls who make a career out of scheming and conning old women. And all for their own eventual financial benefit. The stories I've heard. Revolting!"

"Oh, come down off your soapbox, Belinda," came Mitchell's amused and sarcastic voice. "You're making a mountain out of a molehill, can't you see? Aunt Priscilla is fine, and Hillary is delightful, and you, my dear, are a mental case."

The doctor made no comment.

"There may be a bit to what Belinda says, Mitchell," came Arnold's catlike purr. "She's called the lawyer, you know, to make the will. That Hillary has wasted no time."

"So' far, I've seen no sign of a lawyer on the doorstep. If you ask me—" Mitchell said.

"The lawyer will be here next week. He's been out of town." A silence came over the room.

"How do you know that?" Mitchell's voice was barely above a whisper.

"I, er, overheard. I just happened to lift the receiver in the other room when Hillary called the attorney. I couldn't help but hear."

Hillary was so angry, standing alone in the foyer outside of the room, she wanted to scream. How dared they carry on like that! Making accusations, listening in on private phone calls, showing constant concern for their own place in Priscilla's future will.

She didn't know what to do. Half of her wanted to fling herself away from the door, to ignore and try to forget the hurtful words she had heard bandied about in the same breath as her own name. But it wasn't fair to be so unjustly accused. It wasn't true. The other side of her spitfire personality was in a rage, spurred on, most probably, by the champagne that was still mingled in her bloodstream. It was bad enough that Dr. Newburg had heard such malicious things said about her. But Kent Harris was in that room, too, and that thought stung with a piercing deepness that she had never felt before. Her temper won out. She crossed the stone floor in angry strides and pushed open the ornate doors that had been ajar.

The room before her fell into silence and she faced the group with her eyes aflame.

"I guess you could say that Arnold is not the only eavesdropper here," she began in a low, calm voice. "On my way to this room, I couldn't help but overhear the interesting subject you were discussing."

Mitchell stood up and crossed over to her.

"Now, Hillary, don't be mad. Some of them were just airing their fears, their doubts. No one's really accused you of anything. And you know how I feel about all of this."

Her flashing eyes made him stop.

"To say that I am totally innocent in this whole fiasco would be a waste of breath, I am sure. But I am. And I don't care what you think of me. My intentions are only to have Priscilla Scott well and back to her former health. But I can't speak for your intentions."

Her eyes traveled around the room. The Highfields were sitting together on the sofa, their faces alike in their looks of suspicion and hate. Arnold Weaver sat almost coyly, his legs crossed in an easy chair, regarding her through eyes that were like slits. No need to wonder what he thought. Mitchell looked miserable, his offhand charm at a loss. For once, he stood shifting his weight from one foot to another. He clearly didn't know what to think.

Dr. Newburg sat back in an overstuffed chair, his glasses low on his nose, and regarded her with the look of a man who was taking in all that was going on around him.

At least, Hillary thought fleetingly, he knows Priscilla. He knows about these relatives. He'll be fair.

But it was Kent Harris that almost broke her heart. He was detached from the group, standing with his back to the conversation that shot like bolts of lightning through the room, his dark eyes gazing out into the blackness of the night through the large windows that faced the ocean. He gave no sign of believing the wild ideas of the family, which might, under normal circumstances, have been a comfort to Hillary. But standing alone, amidst all the faces in the room, with no one rushing to her defense or understanding her unfair plight, she felt his lack of response was like hostility. It was as if he were shouting out to her that he agreed with the others.

She felt miserable. "I think you're horrible. All horrible! And I can't help but hope that none of you will ever benefit from Miss Scott's estate. You are the most selfish and unfair people that I've ever laid eyes upon!"

She flung herself out of the living room as the last of her words fell from her shaking lips, swinging the doors behind her. As she entered the foyer, the sight of the large front door before her seemed a haven, an escape from the pain and confusion that was overflowing from her heart.

She opened the black door with tears in her large green eyes and fled thankfully into the cool night air.

Chapter 10

The breeze that drifted in over the ocean worked like a slap in the face for Hillary's raging mind, an instant plunge back into reality, a tonic for her ragged nervous system.

She drew a deep breath of the fresh air, and silently and carefully picked her way along the dark path that led to her favorite spot on the ocean cliffs. The night was very black around her, the moon hidden behind clouds in the summer sky, the stars not even in sight overhead.

It was the first time she had ventured outside of the thick castle walls after dark, and she found it eerie and more than a bit lonely. But she did not turn back, and made her way slowly as her green eyes grew accustomed to the lack of light.

She jumped with fright for an instant, as something warm and soft brushed against her ankle. But she berated herself for her absurdly silly behavior when a hard look revealed that it was only Percival who accompanied her. The black cat brushed against her affectionately, and she felt more relaxed for his company.

She reached the rocky seat that had been such a spot of contentment for her, and gazing out over the darkness of the ocean, she tried to sort out her troubled thoughts and mixed-up emotions.

There was no way that she could clear her name from suspicion in the eyes of the household members, without laying her life bare before them, telling them the set of circumstances that had led her to Eagle's Watch and Priscilla Scott. And that she was not willing to do. It did not matter, in reality, what they thought of her, as long as Scotty herself knew and understood the situation and did not share in their thoughts. But it would make her life so much easier if Scotty would announce her plans for the sharing of the estate, to remove any traces of the doubt that they had about her.

Kent. He had not even given her so much as a glance as she had faced those adamant accusers. He had not even seemed to care about her guilt or innocence. Hillary tried to recapture the moment that she had entered the dining room, the moment when she had shared the glow that had emanated from his eyes. But it seemed an eternity ago. It seemed a dream. Things had changed in the meantime, and she was at a loss to know what to do about it.

It was a very unsettling thought to know that almost all of the people that surrounded you would be happier if you were not there. In her mind, Hillary saw the ugly red word LEAVE scrawled across her mirror once more. Which one of them had written it? It could have been any of them. It could have been all of them.

She reached down and stroked the well-groomed back of Percival, and he responded with a resounding purr.

"At least you're on my side, Percival. You and Scotty. I guess I will have to be satisfied with that." And perhaps in time, some of the other members of the household would see that her intentions were good. She tried to raise her hopes, but the thought of Kent Harris's broad back as he turned away from her blotted out any progress her morale was making.

The chill of the night was beginning to reach her bones. The thin material of her dress was no shelter from the biting sea air that blew across the top of the cliff. She could not stay in this spot any longer. The time had come to return to the castle. Hopefully, she could avoid any further confrontations with those she did not wish to see.

She stood up to begin her return along the path. At that instant, the sound of a yowl reached her ears, making the hairs on the back of her neck stand out, making a chill run the entire length of her spine.

Percival. Never before had she heard the cat utter such a noise—so angry, so aggressive.

She spun around to see what had caused him to react in such a way. And then it happened.

Something hit her. The force caught her right in the back of the knees, like a none-too-subtle football tackle. It sent her sprawling forward, totally off balance, totally out of control.

She felt her heart rise high into her dry throat, as her body hurled several feet forward, her mind screamingly conscious of the edge of the cliff looming before her in the silent darkness of the night.

She was going over the edge, and there was nothing she could do about it. She opened her mouth and tried to scream, a last-ditch effort to protest the horrible fate that she saw undeniably before her. But no sound would come out. Her mind was frozen, her vocal cords were paralyzed. This was the end.

* * *

But it was not the end. As she closed her petrified eyes, her body felt a searing sword of pain. Something had broken her fall. She was still far above the crashing sound of the waves at the bottom of the cliff.

Indeed, she had gone over the edge, to what surely looked like a plummet to a horrible death. But as if by a miracle, she had been caught against a rough and jagged plateau of rock that jutted out a few feet from the almost sheer cliffside. She had fallen almost ten feet, she saw in amazement, as she strained her eyes to calculate the distance to the top of the cliff.

The throbbing in her leg brought her mind back to practical matters. She had been injured in the perilous fall, but was, she realized with a sudden burst of amazement, much better off than she would ever have dreamed possible.

She shuddered as her eyes wandered to the darkened waves breaking on the rocks below. She looked away quickly, vowing to keep her equilibrium in a situation that was still far from settled.

The ledge she had landed on was far too small for much maneuvering, and so she inspected her battered body the best she could while clinging to the rough stone wall behind her. Her ankle was swelling rapidly, but she suspected that the damage was a sprain, rather than a break, as she could still move her foot about, if a bit uncomfortably. Her legs were scraped, and she felt the warm wetness of blood running down her right cheek from a surface wound near her hairline. Her dress was torn to rags.

She would be fine, she consoled herself as she huddled on that little slip of a ledge, feeling the cold air whip around her tousled red hair. Fine, that is, as soon as she could once again find her feet on the solid ground that was now so many feet above her head.

She tried to use her voice again. "Help!" she called with all of the strength she could muster. "Help!" The sound of the waves below her, coupled with the force of the wind, drowned out the feeble attempt. What could she do?

And then Percival saved the day. High above, on the edge of the cliff, she heard him howling at the top of his lungs. The sound was ear-splitting and nerve-grating, but it certainly did its job. In a very few moments, she heard rapid footsteps on the path above her.

"It's the cat. Listen to him! What on earth is the matter with him?" They tried to shoo him away unaware of the cat's single-minded intent. But he would not be stilled.

"Help!" cried Hillary with all of her remaining strength. "Down here! Over the cliff!"

Three dark silhouettes appeared above her.

"Good heavens!" came Kent's deep voice. "It's Hillary! Are you all right?"

"What on earth happened?" Mitchell sounded dazed.

"I say now. This is a problem." Even Arnold's voice was a welcome sound.

Kent sprang into action.

"Get ropes," he ordered the two men and called to the others, who were further down the path, "warm blankets. Hot coffee! It's darn cold out here. She's going to need some attention when we get her up."

Before much more time had passed, Kent's dark figure appeared over the edge of the cliff, a thick rope knotted securely around his waist.

"Kent, are you sure you want to go down there?" Dr. Newburg's voice was questioning.

"I'm sure." He made his way down the side of the darkened cliff. "More light," he called to the group at the top. And then he reached her.

There was scarcely room for his feet to stand safely on the life-saving ledge that supported her, but he managed to balance long enough to tie an additional rope around her now almost limp form and pull her to her feet.

She cried out in pain as her foot tried to support her weight.

"Just relax, Hillary," came his voice, moments ago so strong and forceful, now suddenly soft and calm. "I'll take care of you."

His broad arms scooped her into his with a single action as he lifted her gently and instructed her to hold on to his shoulders.

"All right," he called to the top. "Let's go."

The trip up was, as she heard later, a risky and treacherous one. But to Hillary, leaning so totally on Kent's strong form, and in a mild state of shock, it was a deliverance.

She was rushed to the house, where Mrs. Raymond bustled about her, removing the remains of her once striking dress and pulling a warm flannel bathrobe tightly around her thin figure. She sat in one of the comfortable living-room chairs, under a pile of blankets, while many hands plied her with hot coffee and tried to be solicitous.

Dr. Newburg quickly and efficiently wrapped her painful ankle and bandaged her wounds. Kent stood by his side, and she noticed him flexing the fingers of his right hand as he watched.

"How terribly unfortunate," came Belinda's high-pitched voice. "What a terrible accident."

Arnold was less patronizing. "Really, Hillary, you should be more careful than to climb about on those horrible cliffs at night. Especially in a dress like that. No wonder you fell."

Something inside of her snapped.

"Who did this to me?" she cried out in rage. "Who pushed me?" She distinctly remembered the hold around her legs, the unmistakable feeling that a human force had started her descent. "I swear I was pushed."

The eyes that stared back into hers were wide and shocked. Silence filled the room.

"Certainly, she's upset. Isn't she, Doctor? Perhaps we should get her right up to bed." Belinda sounded strained and upset.

"I'm fine. But I was pushed. By someone who doesn't want me around here."

"Perhaps it was the cat, Hillary," Arnold suggested. "He's awfully high-strung, according to Mrs. Raymond. Perhaps he bumped into you on the trail of a mouse or some such thing. I really don't think that anyone here would "

"Think what you like," Hillary stormed. "But someone doesn't want me around here. Someone also stole into my room the other day and defaced the mirror with a message for me to leave. Was that the cat, too?"

The doctor cleared his throat. "Well, I don't think we are going to be able to solve any of this at this hour of the night and I know that you, young lady, must go to bed right now. You've had a narrow and extremely harrowing escape, whatever caused it. And if you don't want any more ill effects, I prescribe instant rest and quiet. And that's an order."

His voice was quiet and mellow, but its message came firmly across to Hillary, who knew herself that his medical advice was very sound. Besides, she was weary.

She nodded numbly, and Dr. Newburg motioned to Mr. Raymond to help her up to her room. She went willingly, her heart still not emptied of the anger and fear that had been planted within it, like a fertile seed. She noticed, with a twinge of pain, as she was taken from the living room, that Kent Harris was once again standing at the window on the far side of the room, his back once again facing her heavy heart.

Chapter 11

Hillary opened her eyes to a bright and sunny day, but with the aches and pains that emanated from almost every part of her body, her mood was less than ecstatic. She gently raised herself from her usually comfortable bed and looked in the mirror to survey the damage done by her escapade.

The white bandage that Dr. Newburg had applied so efficiently to her temple stood out like a white flag. Her cheekbone sported a very unattractive bruise. Her eyes were underlined by dark circles, and their usual sparkle was lacking.

Her legs were scratched and bruised, but her tightly wrapped ankle was much improved from its condition the night before. She gingerly put a little weight on it, feeling the soreness still, but able to move about with care.

Scotty would be waiting for her in the next room, she knew, having slept soundly through all of the excitement, and she was probably going to flip when she saw Hillary's battered appearance. And what should she tell her?

On the one hand, she longed to howl loudly and long about her definite knowledge that someone had deliberately caused her to fall over the edge of the cliff. She longed to make enough noise about the incident, so that she was finally believed and listened to.

But because she cared so deeply for Scotty, her hands were tied. The idea that someone had knowingly brought harm to Hillary, the fact that she might have easily been killed in her fall from the cliffs of Eagle's Watch, would be too much for her old heart to bear.

The young nurse thought of Scotty's piercing eyes and always working mind. She would have to be told about the incident. Her probing curiosity would eventually win out. But, Hillary realized with a sigh, she would have to agree solemnly with the others, say that the whole thing had been a freak accident. She could make no more accusations for Scotty's sake. She must let the matter die down. It was not a welcome decision, but if she did not wish to risk a flare-up in Scotty's heart condition, she really had no choice.

And so she appeared in Scotty's room a few minutes later, smiling sheepishly, and apologetically told her tale of accidental woe to explain the cuts and bruises and limp.

And those bright eyes stared directly into hers, remarking sarcastically on Hillary's lack of coordination as she took her daily dose of medicine and routinely went through her morning exercise program.

The subject of conversation gradually changed, and Hillary breathed easier as she felt removed from Scotty's scrutinizing gaze. The crisis had been averted.

Dr. Harris appeared at the door to Scotty's room in late morning, alone and carrying his black doctor's bag. He looked handsome and professional, and Hillary's heart gave its customary lurch.

"I'm making a few calls for Dr. Newburg," he said. "I thought I'd drop by to see that things are running smoothly here." He examined Priscilla, and then made a quick check of Hillary's injuries.

"I've been telling Scotty how clumsily I almost came to an unfortunate end last night." Hillary's voice was light and flip, but her eyes sent out the serious message that she had not mentioned her accusations to her patient. "I must thank you for your gallant rescue. It could have been a tragic accident."

His eyes looked into hers for a moment, reading the thoughts that were behind her words.

"Very," he said quietly. He picked up his bag. "Hillary, Dr. Newburg has decided that Scotty is ready for some new therapy equipment at this point, and he suggested that you and I drive down to pick it up in town. If you can come along, it can be demonstrated for you. I thought perhaps late this afternoon, if that's convenient for you—unless your foot is bothering you too much..."

A broken leg wouldn't have stopped her.

"That would be fine, Doctor. I'll be expecting you."

She kept her voice professional and calm, but her stomach was in a state of frenzy.

She and Scotty followed their normal routine. Somehow the hours passed.

Hillary had just settled her patient down for her afternoon nap and had slipped into a cool, stylish pantsuit when Mrs. Raymond arrived to inform her that the doctor was waiting.

She moved down the long stairway with her happy feet barely touching the steps.

The ride to town was a beautiful one, the greenery that lined the roads reflecting the late afternoon sunshine. The July sun had baked the macadam road they traveled, and she could see the waves of escaping heat hovering over the blackened tar as they moved along the curves and hills at a steady pace.

Kent sat in the driver's scat of his car, a bronze-colored sedan that rode smoothly and effortlessly, so different from Hillary's battered VW. She stared occasionally at his strong profile, entranced by it.

"Dr. Newburg is very impressed with the progress you've been making with Priscilla, Hillary. He says that her leg and arm strength are improving to the point that we can add the use of a few weight-lifting devices, and very possibly the use of a walker in the near future."

Hillary could feel a glow beginning deep in her heart. She envisioned Scotty, once again on her feet, with the help of a walker at the start; a positive, rewarding step that would gladden her heart.

Kent smiled at the softened look on her face, and she turned her head away under his gaze.

"You really do care for her, don't you, Hillary?" he asked finally. She nodded.

"And that's why you were so careful to stress that last night's occurrence came under the category of accident."

"I didn't see that I had any choice, as things stand. It would have only hurt her, and I could never prove it."

He nodded silently.

"How did you come to take this job. Hillary? Have you known Priscilla long?"

A little voice spoke silently deep inside her: Don't misjudge me as the others do. Please don't wonder about my motives.

Out loud she merely said. "A friend recommended me for the job, so I took it."

He seemed to accept her words.

"Do you live with Dr. Newburg?" she asked then.

He laughed and she liked the sound of it. "No, no, I'd have to be a lunatic to live with him. He works more hours than there are in a day. I swear I don't have any idea how he does it all, and still keeps on his feet.

"Besides his patient load, and the local needs at every hour of the day and night, he spends the rest of his time hidden deep in a little laboratory he's had built onto the back of his house. He's been devoted to research since his earliest days in medicine and more willingly gives up his sleep than his cherished time in his laboratory. I hope the day comes when he can dedicate himself totally to it. He's a man with a lot to contribute to the world. And he certainly has a soft spot in his heart for Priscilla Scott. Miss Scott has always believed in him, and encouraged him to go on. I believe in him, too."

She was impressed by the reverence in his voice. "Perhaps with you as an associate, he'll feel less pressed for time. Are you planning to stay?"

Kent's muscular hands gripped the wheel of the car with sudden intensity. "We'll see," he said through a tight jaw. Subject closed. She had hit upon a raw nerve.

A few moments of uncomfortable silence hung over them until he spoke again.

"I'm living in the old lighthouse that juts out into the sea beyond Eagle's Watch. The keeper lives in a little cottage that sits next to it, and he offered me space in the lighthouse for my bachelor quarters, in return for taking medical care of his ailing wife. It suits me fine, for now. I'm a city fellow, though. It's a little remote. It'll take getting used to." She knew the feeling.

Bachelor quarters. The words sounded good as they rang in her brain. He was unmarried.

They reached the medical-supply center in town and busily inspected and selected from the large line of rather dusty stock. In no time at all, they had made the necessary purchases and loaded the car with their packages.

The ride home was uneventful, a quiet, peaceful ride.

But the happiness was marred by the occasional throbbing of her ankle and the terrifying memory of how she had gone hurtling over the jagged cliff.

The days passed. And then the weeks. Scotty was amazing. With the drive and determination that Hillary had noticed on their first meeting, she had taken on and conquered each step of her recovery. Day after day, hour after hour, the two had worked together on each muscle-building exercise.

Scotty's muscle tone was good now, and her self-confidence was building with each success that she made. She was getting stronger.

The day that she first stood in her walker was a proud and joyful one. Her arms shakily supported her weight as she lifted herself from the chair, determination etched on her face, with Hillary standing nearby. From that point on, both patient and nurse knew that the success they both yearned for could be a reality.

Hillary had not seen much of Kent in the lazy days that followed their trip for supplies, but he was still very much on her mind. Dr. Newburg came by only occasionally now, as Scotty was far along on her road to recovery.

In the evenings, after Scotty retired for the night. Hillary would sit alone in her room, reading book after book of the delightful poetry borrowed from the well-stocked shelves in the study downstairs.

Looking out in the dark of the night, from her room on the second floor of the castle, she could see the wandering beam of the lighthouse making its mark across the blackness of the sky. Kent's lighthouse.

Sitting in the solitude of her quiet room, she found great comfort in knowing that he was living there, beneath the steady beam of light that crossed the sky.

He was so quiet, so handsome, a man she could sense felt deeply and strongly about life. She knew that there was much his mind knew, that there had to be deep reasons and feelings to account for his sometimes withdrawn behavior. She thought of him often, hoping that the day would come when she would be able to understand the man she cared for so greatly.

On one bright sunny afternoon, while Scotty was comfortably napping, Hillary changed into a comfortable pair of jeans and donned her sneakers, yearning for the fresh air outside the walls of the castle and the peaceful rhythm of the waves along the shore.

She would take no more chances climbing around on the rocky uneven cliffs in shoes that had no tread, for the memory of her fearful night still haunted her.

But since that night, there had been no more suggestions of danger. Even the talk of the incident had died a quick death with her decision to regard it as an accident. Though she knew better, she could almost wish it had been—as they had all easily assumed—a figment of her overactive imagination.

She left the house in good spirits and almost immediately ran into Mitchell. Soon they were weaving in and out of the large rock formations that surrounded Eagle's Watch on three sides. It was exhilarating to climb high in the sunlight, feeling the heat on her back.

But when Mitchell suggested that they scramble down the rocky path that began far behind the castle and led to a small sandy beach, she was more than a little apprehensive. She finally agreed, though.

When she arrived at the bottom, she was more than glad that she had steeled herself to make the trip. The sandy stretch of beach that opened before them was a very small one, a semi-sheltered little place with walls of rock acting as shields on three sides, barring the wind. It was peaceful and lovely. A spray of the fresh salt air touched her freckled face as Mitchell took her hand and drew her to a comfortable spot in the sand. They sat together, laughing and talking for quite some time, Mitchell's voice gay, his easy laugh ringing over the sound of the waves. Hillary felt relaxed, at home. She was glad she had come, she was glad she had a friend like Mitchell. She looked over at his dark-skinned profile as he gazed out at the horizon, his wavy dark hair dipping over one eye, his body relaxed and natural. Never, she knew now, could she feel the same about him as she did about Kent, never could she love him. And yet she liked his company, enjoyed being with him. She liked his easy laugh, his cheerful disposition. He was a friend. So they sat and laughed in the peace of the day, tossing shells and pebbles into the tumult of the ocean, watching the rise and fall of the waves on the small beach.

"You're really something else, Hillary," he said, as they were getting ready to climb to the top once again. He put his hands on her shoulders and pulled her closer to him.

Her muscles tensed. She didn't want more than his friendship.

But Mitchell smiled. "No, Hillary, don't worry, I can see how the land lies. And it's okay, really. You're a very special girl, maybe just too special for the likes of me. But I just want you to know how much I care about you, as a person, as a friend." His voice was warm. "I am your friend, Hillary, remember that." He leaned over and kissed her lightly on her cheek.

She felt warm and happy, a gentle glow inside her as she smiled back at him. "Thanks, Mitchell. You've made my day."

She felt as bright as the sun as they climbed the path upward. It had been a good day.

But as Hillary raised her eyes to judge the distance to the top, she could feel a dense layer of clouds settling over her happy emotions. For at the top of the cliff, unnoticed by Mitchell, Hillary could see the glint of sunlight reflecting off a head of very blond hair. Daisy, the quiet housemaid, was perched up on the rocks above, watching, without a doubt, the two of them on the path. The look in the golden little face, usually marked with its wide-eyed innocence, its delicate beauty, was far from a friendly one. Eyes were knowing now, dark and flashing, the chin hard with anger.

Hillary looked down to check her progress on the rocky slope, and when she again raised her eyes to the ledge, Daisy was gone.

But why had she been spying on them on the beach? What had she wanted to see? It didn't make sense, Hillary's mind argued. It was probably nothing at all. But it had given Hillary an insight into the sprightly blonde who lived within the walls of Eagle's Watch, and that insight was not a happy one. If the look Hillary had seen had been meant for her, then one more person at Eagle's Watch was not exactly delighted with her presence.

And why for heaven's sake? A little shiver traveled the length of her spine. The fears that she had been trying to put to sleep were rising up again with force. She felt as if a giant web were being spun around her, slowly, quietly, and that sooner or later it would tighten and stifle her completely.

Chapter 12

"I have a peculiar feeling that that new housemaid, Daisy, doesn't care much for me," Hillary said conversationally to Scotty the next day as she helped her move her walker across the floor of her room. The process was an exhausting experience for Scotty, but one that was a labor of love. For each day the task became less strenuous and her progress grew more and more evident.

"I'm not surprised," laughed Scotty when she paused for a well-earned break. "I imagine that Mitchell—if I know him as well as I think I do—hasn't been above making a pass or two at our perky little blonde in the short time that she's been here. She's most probably as jealous as can be every time she sees him throw a look in your direction. Mitchell is not very—well, shall we say, discreet?"

"But there's nothing at all between Mitchell and me. We're just friends. There's no reason for her to be jealous at all."

"Well, I know that, and you know that, and Mitchell knows that, though I'm sure he wishes it otherwise. But Daisy McClintock doesn't know that, and what's more, I doubt that she'd believe it if she heard it. She's the type that thrives on jealousy. I think you'll find."

"How you come up with your crazy insights about personalities, I'll never know. But you're probably right, Scotty, as usual."

"It's easy to see that Mitchell is not your type of man, Hillary, too flighty and easygoing. Not enough moral fiber, not enough drive. You need a more intense man, with deeper feelings, a strong feeling of right and wrong. More like that handsome Dr. Harris, I'd say."

Hillary blushed to the roots of her already red hair, and her pulse quickened as it always did at the thought of Kent Harris.

"I can't see that I've made much of a lasting impression on him, Scotty. He hasn't exactly been beating down the castle door in his haste to get here to see me."

"He's simply a man with other pressing things on his mind. You've simply got to get around them, that's all."

Hillary stared at her and shook her head. "Simply? Just how would you suggest that I go about that?"

Scotty laughed deeply. "That, my dear, is up to you. But I shouldn't think you'd have too much of a problem. Use your heart, and your God-given brain, girl. I can't see how anyone in their right mind would dislike you, Hillary."

"I don't seem to make friends very easily in this household. Everyone seems to have some kind of reason to dislike me. It's a very unsettling feeling."

"Bah. If you live life to the fullest, you are bound to ruffle some feathers, my dear. You can't let a few sideward glances get the better of you. You know how the old rhyme goes. Sticks and stones may break your bones, but names will never hurt you."

Hillary suppressed a shiver as she recalled her painful moments, paralyzed on the cliff. Her lack of "broken bones" was only a quirk of fate.

Scotty was quick to pick up on her reaction. "What's troubling you, Hillary? Are you frightened about something?"

"No, no, of course not," she reassured her quickly, hoping she sounded convincing. Scotty was as perceptive as a hawk, but Hillary was determined to keep from worrying her.

When she left Scotty settled down for her afternoon rest that day, she left with a knot in the pit of her stomach. She had come close to baring the facts that she wanted to hide, close to letting her feelings of fear and anxiety show through. She had stilled Scotty's questions, she had recovered her composure, but she had been very aware of the way her patient's sharp old eyes followed her movements around the room, the way her brow knitted together as it did when she was deep in thought. Hillary prayed earnestly that Scotty was not reading her mind, as she so often did.

The lawyer finally arrived. He appeared at the big black entrance to the foyer of Eagle's Watch, briefcase in hand, and after very few words, was ushered up to Scotty's room. He was old and small in size, rather like a shriveled fruit that is left on the vine. His manner was gruff and efficient and he gave off the aura of dry, dusty lawbooks, with no apparent sense of humor.

Hillary remained behind in the living room as Mrs. Raymond accompanied him up the stairs. The young nurse hoped that Scotty's final decision about her will would ease the tensions in the house considerably.

Hillary had every intention of convincing Scotty to make her decision known, make the facts public and remove the mystery and suspicion that seemed to be hovering over the castle.

She collapsed into one of the large stuffed chairs and put her head back to relax. But her rest didn't last long.

"Happy with yourself, I imagine!" Belinda's sharp voice cut through the air of the once-quiet living room.

Hillary blinked her eyes open to see the portly figure in its brightly colored dress crossing the rug toward her rather unceremoniously. She shouldn't, Hillary thought instinctively, wear red. She looked distinctly like a fire engine. In fact, there was fire in her eyes.

"Well, Nurse Holt, I suppose you could say, mission accomplished. In a short while the will will be sealed, signed, and delivered." She paused, but the rage in her eyes screamed on. Hillary swallowed, not quite sure how to counter the angry accusation that Scotty's niece was making.

She decided to hang on to her temper. "Belinda," she said quietly and evenly, "I have no reason to believe that Scotty would even mention my name in her will, and I swear that I want no part of it."

"A very easy thing to say, at this point." Belinda's eyes narrowed as she spoke. "And why else would you be waiting on her, hand and foot, all smiles and good-natured? Rather more than mere devotion to duty, isn't it?"

It was more than duty, Hillary knew, but the difference was one that would be lost on Belinda. It was friendship, it was caring, it was a kind of love, and it had nothing to do with dollar signs or wills.

"Did it ever occur to you that I might care for Scotty? That she might be more than a patient to me?"

"Harumph" snorted Belinda. She shook her head angrily and left the room. Hillary was far from sorry to see her go.

The lawyer appeared again, asking for Daisy and Annie, whom Scotty had selected to be witnesses to the signing of her will. The two were quickly called from the kitchen—Daisy, lithe and light; Annie, puffing and tired as they climbed the steps to Scotty's room.

Hillary moved into the hallway and started toward the kitchen, hoping to find a snack before returning to her duties upstairs. Arnold Weaver was moving along the passageway toward her, and she had no alternative but to meet him in the hallway.

"My, my, and here's the little Florence Nightingale of Eagle's Watch." His very being stirred up an instant feeling of dislike and contempt in her, but she suppressed it with effort.

After all, perhaps they would all find out in the near future about Scotty's plans for the distribution of her property.

"I'm sorry I don't have time to stop and chat, Mr. Weaver," she said in a voice so controlled that it surprised even herself. "I was just on my way to get a quick snack for myself."

"Celebrating, eh?" he said in his affected voice. "Let me tell you something, young lady. If you have cheated us out of what is rightfully ours, you are going to be very, very sorry."

He moved quickly and silently on, leaving Hillary to stare open-mouthed at his receding back. A threat?

She no longer had any desire to eat. Her stomach was suddenly in a tight little ball. The tenseness and suspicion in the house was having a deep effect on her. And Arnold Weaver gave her the creeps. She thought came to her that he was the closest relative, the one to inherit everything if Scotty died without a will. How it must unsettle him to know the will was being made this very minute, that he might have lost it all. Lost it to Hillary, he thought, though she knew that that wasn't the case. No wonder he hated her so. Enough to kill? She remembered the very human touch she had felt on the night she had been hurtled over the cliff.

Someone had wanted her out of the way, and the will hadn't even been written yet.

And now? If the person who had attempted to get rid of her feared that she was to inherit, what would be the logical next step? To insure that Hillary was to die before Scotty, leaving the inheritance available once again to the greedy relatives.

"You will be very sorry." Arnold Weaver had said. A chill settled over her. Suddenly, she knew she had to talk to Scotty, had to convince her to explain her intentions to her family.

She passed the lawyer on her way up the stairs. He nodded and left by the front door, his flat black briefcase holding the now all-important document.

She tapped lightly on Scotty's door and went in.

"Ah, Hillary, just the person I wanted to see. Well, it's all done, sealed, signed, and delivered. That's a load off of my mind."

"Scotty," Hillary began nervously, "don't you, ah, think that you could call the family together and explain the terms that you've decided on? It would make everyone much more well, comfortable."

She fought for the right words, always aware that to hint of the danger that she felt in the air would upset her patient too much, would risk her progress, and even threaten her life.

"No, no, Hillary, I've no intention of doing any such thing. Call it an old woman's whim. A little anxiety won't do them any harm." Her eyes were dancing. She was enjoying her position of power.

"But it's so difficult for me to cope with them," Hillary pleaded. "It would make it so much easier..."

But Scotty shook her head.

"I have my reasons," the nurse went on.

"And don't imagine that you can tell them either, Hillary. After all, how can you be sure that I didn't do just as they expect? You know how impulsive I am."

Hillary stared at her open mouthed. Scotty couldn't have. She couldn't have!

But Scotty only laughed. "I swear. Hillary, you look as if you'd seen a ghost. Just forget about the will. I just don't wish to make my decisions known yet." ~

She looked very tired, so Hillary tucked her in for a rest.

As much progress as Scotty was making, the emotional strain of the morning with the lawyer had left their mark, and Hillary knew that her impulse to hide her suspicions from Scotty was right. But she'd have to talk to someone. She'd have to find an answer. She had hoped so much that the tensions would be over when the will had been written, but she had been mistaken. It looked as though they were just beginning.

As Scotty's strength was building steadily with each passing day, Hillary decided that the time had come to once again introduce the idea of returning to the beloved sculpturing that she loved so well. On the first occasion that it had been brought up, her patient had stated, loud and clear, that she would have to be able to walk to the turret room before she would try her hand once again—and now that time was just around the corner.

Scotty could move her sturdy walker around her room with a growing sense of security. Developing the strength and skills to climb the tower steps would be next. And Hillary instinctively felt that the sooner it was attempted, the better. It would be a major step in convincing Scotty that she was once again well and able to cope with the world. The thought sent a surge of excitement through Hillary. She decided to travel the long way to the studio turret, to judge the difficulty Scotty would have maneuvering her way up the steps. Her feet took her down the long upper corridor, deep into the back of the castle, where she pulled open the heavy wooden door that led to Scotty's artist's turret.

It looked different in the daylight, more real than it had appeared on that night that she had explored the castle for the first time. The stone walls that stood waist high were rough and gray, the floor smooth from the ages of footsteps that had continued to cross it. Small splatters of brownish red clay hovered in the cracks in the floor, evidence of the hours of work that the castle's current mistress had put in here.

The center table had a much-used, loved look, as though it were waiting with anticipation for the day when the mounds of clay would rise from the surface again, under the skillful hands of Priscilla Scott, to become expressive creations, much like the ones that filled the low shelves along the wall.

Above the stone wall, large panes of clear glass formed windows all the way around the high round turret. The view in all directions was magnificent, an eagle's look at the world that surrounded the castle. On one side, the ocean in its greenish-blue glory stretched smoothly before Hillary's eyes. She could see the rocks that led up to the castle base. She could see the great expanse of hearty evergreens that grew so abundantly, looking like a plush green carpet that stretched as far as the eye could see. It was beautiful country.

Across the roof of the square and solid castle, Hillary could see the matching turret rising high in the sky. A turret full of shiny armor, a mystery in itself. She looked across at the eerie metal shapes in the far turret that had a way of catching her off guard, making her feel that she was being watched. But then the look froze in her mind. She *was* being watched. For in the other turret, she had seen a definite sign of movement. At least one of the sober shapes that she had thought was armor was alive. Someone was in the turret.

She strained her eyes to see across the distance, but no more movement was apparent. Whoever had been there had gone, and quickly.

Who was it? And why was he there? She was vaguely conscious that her body was beginning to tremble. She hurried down the stone turret steps, with a pounding heart, back to the occupied portion of the castle, away from the shadows and her fears.

The next morning dawned dark and drearily, the rhythm of a million raindrops beating against the glass windows in Hillary's room. The dampness, together with the much cooler temperature, permeated the castle, leaving an uncomfortable chill that matched the mood in Hillary's heart.

She found Scotty with a cold that morning and kept her propped warmly in her bed, protected from the chilled air. She built a cheerful fire in the great stone fireplace that stood proudly at one end of her patient's room, and soon its warmth filled the air pleasantly.

The exercise program was tabled for the day, and Scotty teased Hillary unmercifully about getting a much needed respite from her slave labor.

"I swear, Hillary, it's about time I got a day off. The way you make an old lady work. You should be ashamed of yourself!"

"Nonsense. You're as strong as a horse. But it's best to be cautious with that cold, so I want you to stay calm and rested today. No overexerting at all, and I'm going to give the doctor a ring to see if he wants to prescribe anything to help your sinuses." She left Scotty with a pile of magazines and went downstairs.

Hillary made her phone call to Dr. Newburg's office from the study, listening, with a feeling of frustration, to the repeated ringing in her ear as the phone went unanswered. The doctor was not at home. But just as she was about to replace the receiver, the voice of the town's one operator came over the wire.

"Dr. Newburg is out on calls," she said. "But he'll be checking in with me periodically. Can I take a message?"

"This is Nurse Holt at Eagle's Watch. I wanted to consult with him about Miss Scott, but it's no emergency. Perhaps you could have him call me when he can."

"Consider it done," said the friendly voice on the other end of the line, and Hillary hung up. Life was certainly different here in the country than in the bustling city.

Hillary had no sooner checked on Scotty, finding her sleeping soundly, than Mrs. Raymond announced that Dr. Newburg had just pulled up in the drive.

Hillary ran quickly down the steps to greet him at the door.

"There was no need to get you all the way up here. Doctor," she apologized. "I just called to report to you that Scotty had come down with a cold, and I wanted you to prescribe anything that you felt she should have. She's sleeping now."

"I never mind stopping in on Scotty, Hillary," he said. "She's a very special person to me. Besides, I was on a call out this way when I checked in with the operator, so it wasn't out of my way at all." They walked together into the living room.

"So how long has our little lady been bothered by this cold?"

"Just today, primarily. I kept her in bed and postponed her therapy session, so that she wouldn't overexert herself. Her signs are all normal, but I thought it would be better to be cautious."

"Very wise, Hillary. A cold is not disastrous, but at her age, and in her condition, it could well develop into something more threatening if we weren't careful." He withdrew a prescription pad from his jacket pocket and filled out the top sheet quickly.

"You can get this filled in town," he said. "That should make her more comfortable and not interfere with her other medication. I won't bother her now, since she's sleeping. Just keep her still, as you have so far. And perhaps I'll send Dr. Harris around tomorrow to see how she's faring."

The color rose in Hillary's cheeks at the sound of Kent's name. It didn't go undetected by Dr.

Newburg's observant eyes.

"So what do you think of my new associate. Hillary?"

"Kent? He seems... very nice."

Dr. Newburg laughed out loud. "Your feelings are very transparent, young lady. And I agree with you that he's quite a guy. He's pretty impressed with you, too, if my experienced judgment counts for anything."

She looked in amazement at the gray-haired doctor. "Impressed? He doesn't seem to give me a second look."

"Sometimes, when one looks carefully, one look is all that it takes. Some people just have a harder time than others in opening themselves up to relationships. It's hard to forget the past.

"He's had a rough time. Hillary, I'm afraid his life has been rather overturned lately. And he's just getting over a broken engagement. But time can cure many things, or so they say."

Hillary bit her lip in contemplation. She wished she could deluge the doctor with all of the questions and thoughts about Kent that were constantly racing through her mind. But that wasn't right, she knew. Yet she longed for the time when she could learn more about the man who attracted her so.

"I'm hoping that he'll stay on and help me with my practice. He only came here as a favor to me. He was pretty devastated, and I was hoping that my country medicine might open up a new world for him, as well as give him some time to come to grips with his own mind. Perhaps with a pretty thing like you around, he'll be more likely to stay. Are you planning to keep on with Scotty? She's coming closer and closer to the recovery that you've been working for. Have you discussed the future with her? Any chance of your remaining here?"

Hillary felt a knot in her stomach. Her life had changed so much since she had first arrived at the gray stone castle. She had learned to love Scotty deeply and had lost her heart to the handsome young doctor. But to stay? To stay at Eagle's Watch? It gave her a queer feeling just to think of it.

"I don't think so, Doctor. I came here for a purpose, and I imagine that I'll be moving on once it is fulfilled." She thought of her promise to Miss Matilda, the long overdue debt that she had now nearly repaid. Her life would be her own soon, to do with as she pleased. But now she didn't resent the job that she had taken. It had made her face life, for better or for worse, and her days would hopefully be the better for it. The vision of her beloved hospital rushed before her, the brightly lighted operating room, the surgical feats and successes. She felt her blood surge in her veins.

"And just why did you take this post, Hillary? I have never heard exactly how you came to be in touch with Scotty."

Hillary gave a tired sigh. She had no desire to go into the details and intricacies of Miss Matilda's request.

"I was sent here specifically, for a definite reason, Dr. Newburg, but it really is a personal one, and I don't feel ready to discuss it. At first I wasn't delighted about it, but now I really care for Scotty, and I'm glad I've come." She thought of all the joy that she and Scotty had had together. "I've gotten so much out of knowing her."

The doctor nodded with a preoccupied look on his face. "Fine, fine. Well, I guess I must be running along to finish the rounds I've got lined up for today. I suppose you won't be keeping Dr. Harris here, after all, which is a shame. I certainly wish I could find another such terrific associate. My research is so very important to me, you know. I've had to make great sacrifices to keep it up, and I'm not getting any younger."

"Well, I'm sure you'll find someone, if not Kent, to help you out," she said as she showed him to the door. "And thank you for the prescription. I'll check in on Scotty and then drive to town to fill it. Let's hope tomorrow finds her in better shape."

The doctor climbed into his battered car with a tired air, running a hand through his tousled hair, and Hillary smiled at him and climbed the steps to check on Scotty before joining the others for lunch.

The table seemed a strangely empty place without its white-headed mistress at the head.

The others cornered Hillary almost immediately, their joint voices full of unexpected friendliness. A false kind of concern seemed to drip from their words. It made her more wary of them than their usual hostile behavior.

"Well, Hillary dear," Belinda said patronizingly, "and how is our dear Aunt Priscilla doing these days? Mrs. Raymond mentioned that she has come down with a cold, most unfortunate."

Herman spoke up, a rare occasion. "Maybe you're working her too had, Nurse Holt. She's very old, you know. One must not expect miracles."

"I'm sure Hillary knows what she's doing," Arnold chimed in. "After all, if she succeeds in getting Priscilla back to normal, she'll be a champion. And if she fails—"

Hillary felt the anger rising up within her. "Yes, Mr. Weaver, and if I fail..."

"Then perhaps that failure wouldn't be a failure at all. Perhaps you would benefit even more by pushing Priscilla just a little too hard."

She slammed her fist down on the table and stood up in rage. The will again. They were accusing her of attempting to get her hands on Scotty's money.

"Miss Scott's will is none of my business, nor of yours. She has a right to do whatever she wishes to do with her money. But I must say, if I had scheming relatives like you, I'd think twice about leaving you a penny."

Stillness echoed in the room, and she spun on her heel and moved quickly out the door. In the hallway, Mitchell caught up with her and took her arm.

"Magnificent bit of daring there, Hillary, I must say."

She looked into his laughing eyes and had to smile back.

"You didn't put in your two cents' worth in there, Mitchell. It's not like you to keep out of a conversation."

"I told you before, the issue is over with. Aunt Priscilla is alive and well and in good mental health, from the lashing I periodically receive from her sarcastic tongue, and not at all likely to kick the bucket for some time."

She looked straight into his eyes. "But do you think I have ulterior motives with her? Do you agree with what they have been insinuating?" She was surprised at how desperately she wanted to hear that another human being was on her side.

"Quite frankly, Hillary, no. I don't believe you have any great aspirations to be the next mistress of Eagle's Watch. Actually, I don't think that you are clever enough to think up such a scheme and successfully carry it out." He sounded almost apologetic.

"That's the most lovely compliment I've received all day. Thank you."

"But don't tease them, Hillary. Don't put yourself in a bad position. You'd be playing with fire. There's something funny around here, a tension in the air and I want—well. I want you to take care of yourself."

And with a quick smile he was gone, leaving Hillary with her muddled thoughts and an even greater conviction that all was not well at Eagle's Watch.

Chapter 13

Hillary spent much of the afternoon visiting with Scotty. The rain fell stubbornly until late in the day, leaving everything in sight drenched and dripping, the sharp chill in the air remaining. Later she changed into a comfortable pair of jeans and pulled a thin sweater over her head. She found a yellow mackintosh hanging unused in the downstairs guest closet and sought out Mrs. Raymond to see if she could wear it to drive to town to pick up Scotty's prescription.

"Certainly you may use it, Nurse Holt, it's a spare that we always keep on hand here. When it rains here, it's quite a downpour. But there's no need for you to drive all the way into town. I'm sure Mr. Raymond could make the trip for you."

" Thanks," Hillary said cheerily, happy to hear even these few words of friendliness from the usually sour housekeeper. "But I'm actually looking forward to making the trip. It'll be the first time I've driven my little car since I first pulled up in the drive, and I think I need a little change of atmosphere."

"Whatever you like. But don't be late. Dinner will be at the usual time."

There was a bounce in the girl's walk as she made her way to the almost hidden garage that was nestled amid the boulders in back of the house. Her VW looked forlorn and forgotten.

"If it even starts after all these weeks, it'll be a miracle. Come on, little car," she said as she put her key in the ignition. "We've been through a lot together." The car answered her with a rather shaky rumble from the engine. At least it had started, if a little hesitantly.

She put it into gear.

Driving down the lane to the highway gave her a strange sensation of exhilaration. It was a wonderful feeling to be behind the wheel of her VW again, its familiarity making the problems of the present evaporate quickly. She felt almost as if the events of the last few weeks had never happened, that she had never received the letter from Miss Matilda that had so abruptly changed her life. She had almost paid that debt now. Priscilla Scott would soon be back to her normal, strong self. Hillary could soon make plans to leave the world of Eagle's Watch behind her.

She was filled with mixed emotions. Here in her happy little car, riding pleasantly into town on a simple errand, she enjoyed the gusts of cool, moist air that drifted in the open window. The misgivings and suspicions that she had built up seemed silly and dramatic.

The writing on her mirror had been a harmless prank, one that its performer had been embarrassed to own up to. The push from the cliff, most probably a combination of raw nerves and an overactive imagination. The figure in the tower had probably been one of the servants, guilty only of shirking on the job.

Her mind felt as if it were ceasing to spin for the first time in ages. She was trying to convince herself there was no danger. There was no reason for the nagging feeling of apprehension that had irked her so. In her carefree state of mind, she chided herself for allowing overactiveness of her imagination to color her rational thinking so dramatically. The little car started its descent down the long, twisting road that wound its way to town. There were no other cars on the road. After the day's gusty storm, she had the stretch to herself. She downshifted to maneuver each turn on the steep hill, keeping the car in steady control.

But suddenly, in an unpredictable flash, everything changed. She neared the tightest curve on the road and applied her foot to the brake pedal to slow the car, but her foot went right to the floor. She stomped it again and again, her mind not willing to accept the fact that the brake was not responding. The trickiest part of the curve was fast approaching, and the car wasn't slowing. She could feel her pulse hammering in her ear.

Would she make the turn? She jammed the car into the lowest gear, gritting her teeth and holding the wheel determinedly with white, strained fingers. Her speed lessened and she turned the vehicle with all of her strength. The pavement was slick and wet from the day's storm. Fallen dampened leaves were scattered treacherously before her.

She felt the tires begin to skid beneath her feet. She spun the wheel instinctively to regain control. It made no difference. The car went into a spin. Beads of perspiration appeared on her frightened brow. Her eyes were filled with fear as she thought of the steepness of the rocky, tree-filled hill that she was on. She felt she was a goner.

Thud! The rear of the car connected with a large-trunked tree. The car came to a sudden stop, though her brain still sped on. She rested her face on the wheel before her and attempted to pull her shaky self together. She was safe.

With rubbery legs, she pulled herself out of her little car and went to survey the damage. It began to rain once again as she hugged her borrowed mackintosh close to her. She looked with dismay at the battered car. It seemed to be totally wrecked. The rear had been bashed in by one tree, and the front by another.

But a wave of thanks rolled over her as she looked beyond the car to the rocky expanse below. Only luck had prevented something much worse than a battered car. If she had been moving any faster, if she hadn't been alert to the driving conditions any number of details could have meant her death. Another accident? The case and contentment she had felt in the car were gone. The fear was back. Too many narrow escapes to be dismissed with a shrug!

The sound of a nearing car reached her ears. She stepped into the curving road to warn the coming driver of the wrecked mangle of metal that lay ahead.

It was Kent. His car had barely jerked to a stop before he had flung open the door and pulled himself from behind the wheel.

"Hillary!" he called as he surveyed the situation in a flash. His voice had a raspiness that she had never before heard. He crossed the short distance to where she stood with long strides, and in a split second she felt his big, strong arms encircle her. He did not speak.

In that small space of time, the world righted itself for Hillary. She closed her eyes, feeling the warm nearness of him, and the rain around her seemed to disappear.

He moved his big hands to her shoulders. His eyes stared deeply into hers, and she could read the concern, the worry in them.

"What on earth happened?" he demanded.

"I guess my little car just gave out, finally. The brakes didn't work."

He left her there, midsentence, and before she knew it, she found him half underneath the wreck of a car. She could hear him grunt as he tinkered around.

When he withdrew, his face was gray and long. "I'm afraid that this accident was helped along by a human hand. The brake cable looks as if it has been partially cut through. Using the brakes on that steep hill would be sure to be too much of a strain on it in that condition."

They stood silent in the rain as that fact, and all that it meant, sank in. "Then it was no accident..."

He stared back at her.

"And that night on the cliff..." A shudder traveled the length of her spine. There was no doubt about it. Someone was trying to do away with her.

"Who knew you were taking the car out?" Kent asked abruptly.

"Why, everyone, I guess. Scotty had been in bed with a cold and I was going to town to fill a prescription that Dr. Newburg made up for her."

"The doctor was there?"

"Yes, but she's not really that ill. He says there's nothing to worry about. We're just taking precautions."

"Well, as far as I can see, you'll have to take some precautions about yourself, Hillary Holt. And the first step is to call the police and get you away from here until we find the lunatic who's running around pulling these stunts."

Away! Her heart landed with a thump. The last thing she wanted to do at the moment, danger or not, was to go away from Kent, from Scotty, to leave Eagle's Watch. Not yet.

She remembered the comforting feeling of his arms around her. Surely she would be safe when he was around. She couldn't run away.

"I'm not leaving," she said quietly, watching his eyes carefully to see his reaction. "I have to stay here and take care of Scotty. That's what I came here to do."

"I don't think that dedication to a position requires a sacrifice of your life, Hillary. It's only common sense to go away."

"And never find out the reason for the things that have been happening? I'm not the type to run away."

She saw him wince as soon as her words were out, and she knew she had struck a nerve. Was Kent running away from something, was that part of the burden he carried? She remembered being told there had been a girl.

"Then stay, Hillary, if you're sure that's what you should do. But you've got to be careful and we've got to call the police."

"The police," she said thoughtfully. "I'm so afraid of what all this will do to Scotty. She's bound to think that it's her fault about this will business."

"Do you think that's why you're being attacked? Because you're going to inherit under the will?" His eyes narrowed as he looked at her.

"But I'm not going to inherit under the will," she cried automatically in self-defense. "They only think that I am. But there can't be any other reason, can there?"

"I don't know, Hillary. Only you can answer that one. You've been rather secretive about the circumstances that brought you here."

His words made her temper flare. "I'm not the only one in that category, Kent Harris." How could he make her so happy and then so angry in so short a span of time?

But he answered her blazing eyes with a laugh.

"You certainly are full of spunk, young lady. I'm sorry for my lack of tact. I'm just trying to get at the bottom of this." He reached out and touched her shoulder. "But let me explain a little about myself to you. I'm sorry, Hillary, if I've seemed strange and unreachable since we've known each other. I was moved by you from the first moment that we met that day in the castle. But I've tried to steel myself against any kind of personal involvement." His eyes began to darken.

"It's all right, Kent." She wanted desperately to take the pain out of his eyes.

"No it's not all right. I have to explain. I want to explain. There was a girl, a girl who was very special to me. We were engaged. But it's over. And I'm trying to get my life back together again. But there are answers that I have to find out for myself before I can open a new chapter in my life."

"Are you going to settle here and work with Dr. Newburg?"

"No. At least I don't think so!" His eyes looked distant again.

"But there's some things we have to settle first. Beginning with your safety." He led her to his car.

"We'll have a tow truck take care of the wreckage. I'm afraid there's not much left to salvage."

"Kent, can't we please wait a few more days before we contact the police? I would so much rather figure out this puzzle ourselves than upset Scotty needlessly. And I just don't see what the police could really do in this situation."

He looked at her for a long minute. "Tell me honestly, Hillary, do you have any idea who is responsible for this?"

She shook her head.

"Then you had better take it easy until we find the answers. No car rides, please, and stay off the cliffs. I'm not at all sure we should take this risk."

She quieted him with a smile. "I'll be careful." They rode in silence the rest of the way to Eagle's Watch.

The next two hours were ones of horrendous confusion. Their arrival at Eagle's Watch, with the news of the "accident" sent the house into a turmoil. The tow truck from a local garage reported that there had not been much worth saving from the wreckage, and so Hillary authorized them to haul it away to a junkyard. Belinda and Herman Highfield bustled about in tones of regret and concern, tones that made her bristle because she knew they were not at all founded on real concern.

"I don't want you to breathe even a word that this was not an accident, Kent," she had told him with level eyes as they had arrived at Eagle's Watch. "Scotty would suffer, and it would just put the culprit on guard. I'm going to find out who's behind it."

Kent had grabbed her arm. "I admire your spunk, Hillary, but not your brains. Don't you dare leave yourself open to any more risk or danger. I'll leave you here for now, because I can't really see any alternative, and I'll leave the police out of it, against my better judgment. Meanwhile, I'll do the scouting to find out what this is all about. But you just take care of yourself."

His hand brushed her hair, and she felt as though she was on fire. The memory of the feeling of his arms around her when he had discovered her by the car wreckage made her feel tingly all over.

He stared deeply into her green eyes, his face holding a look of longing, when he left her at the door of the castle to finish the medical rounds that he had been involved with when he had first come upon her. It had been a hasty farewell with promises to keep in touch.

Something was on his mind, she knew, something that was holding his emotions back still. But their relationship had taken a personal turn. The big, husky man that she had come to care for so deeply shared some of the same feeling, she was certain, locked inside of him. And she would find the key to open the door, to make the longing look on his face a reality.

"You should be more careful when you drive, Nurse Holt," was Arnold Weaver's comment. "I've never felt those little foreign cars were safe to drive." He spoke with his usual superior air. "They're a menace on the road. I'd never drive one, that's for certain."

"You'd never drive one because you can't afford to own one," chided Mitchell. "You'd get behind the wheel quick enough if it was free." The two exchanged disgusted looks.

"I hope Hillary isn't pulling these stunts to get attention," said Belinda in her slightly too-loud voice, speaking as though Hillary was not even in the room, despite the fact that she stood only a few feet from her side. "Some girls will do anything for a little attention."

Herman nodded in blind agreement. Herman always agreed with Belinda.

They were an unlikable group, for sure, thought Hillary, but this time she kept herself from reacting to their unmasked barbs. She left the room without an answer and went to tell Scotty the story of the wreck, a slightly altered version, before the hints of it reached her patient's always alert ears.

Chapter 14

"I believe the term is accident prone," Scotty said slyly after hearing Hillary's brief explanation of the wreck of her car. She sat quietly stroking Percival's black shiny coat. "Funny, you don't seem like the accident-prone type to me."

Hillary laughed nervously. "At least my accidents haven't been injurious..." She broke off, stopping herself from adding "yet." She didn't want to think in those terms.

"Yet," Scotty supplied for her. She was staring at Hillary with those clear, knowledgeable eyes, and Hillary felt fidgety inside. Just how much did Scotty know about the things that had been happening?

"I've had a funny feeling that all is not well with my varied guests and employees at Eagle's Watch. And I'm right, Hillary, aren't I? Care to talk to me about it?"

She would have loved to open up and pour out all of the thoughts and ideas that had been plaguing her, to tell her about the accidents, to ask her about the well-cared-for armor in the far turret. She would have loved to tell her of the unhappy state of affairs in her relationship with the family members, to tell her the family was sure that she was here only as a usurper of the Eagle's Watch fortune. But her well-trained medical mind forbade such confidences, knowing that they could possibly upset her patient.

"There's not much to talk about," she said simply. "The general consensus is that I'm a careless idiot, which, I suppose, is not far from the truth."

"Hmm," said Scotty, leaving it at that. Her cold had already begun to subside, and they planned to work together once again the next day. Mr. Raymond arrived with her prescription, having driven to town to get it filled after Hillary's own attempt to do the task had been so horribly thwarted. Scotty took the medicine obligingly.

"I got a letter from Matilda today," she said with a glimmer in her eye.

Hillary stopped short. "Miss Matilda? Is she still in London? How is she?"

"She's fine, just fine. And very glad to hear of the recovery I've been making. I told her about the walker, about the way I can manage almost everything once again. She's very proud of you."

"You are doing marvelously, you know, but it's mostly because of your own determination to work. I've just helped you along a bit."

Scotty reached out a hand and patted Hillary's, which was resting on the bedpost. "You're a very special girl to be here, Hillary. She told me of the job that you had given up, of the plans that you had cancelled in order to come here to take this post. I'm sorry, Hillary. I didn't know.

"But what I wanted to say is this. I'm nearly well now, I know. I have confidence in my strength and can look forward to spending the rest of my days in relatively good health thanks to you. Your duty here is nearly done, you know. I'm freeing you, with Matilda's blessing, to return to the world that you left in order to come here."

There was a large lump in Hillary's throat and she had to pause for a moment before her voice would work. She blinked back the tears that had welled up in her eyes at the old woman's words. How much she cared for Priscilla Scott!

She could go now, she knew. Her patient had come a long way, as she had said. It was only a matter of time before she would be back to "new". And going away would end the mysterious attacks on her life, she knew. She could end her risk here at Eagle's Watch.

And Kent? He had professed no great desire to settle here. In fact, he had seemed almost sure that he could not take over the large practice of Dr. Newburg, so that the doctor could spend more time on his beloved research. Whatever her relationship with Kent would be, it could continue in any location, if their feelings were deep enough. How she prayed that they would be.

But yet, she had to stay. Why? It was difficult to understand, difficult to accept. Was it because leaving Scotty with anyone such as the person who had done these treacherous things would be dangerous? Was it that she herself wanted to bring to justice the person who was her unknown enemy? Or was it just her never-ending need to fulfill her duties, to tie up all the ends in one part of her life before going on with the next chapter? But whatever the reason, she knew that she was not leaving, at least not yet.

The operating tables of the great hospitals would still be there when everything was cleared up at Eagle's Watch.

"Sorry, Scotty, you just can't get rid of me yet. I'm staying." She tucked her in and walked out the door, full of determination to succeed in her pursuits.

And Scotty's eyes followed her, glistening with tears, watching the young girl who had come to mean so much to her.

Hillary felt very thoughtful as she slipped lightly down the steps, going by the staring portraits of Scotty's ancestors. It was nearing the dinner hour, and she longed for a few quiet minutes to pull herself together before facing the ever-continuing pressure that was inevitable at the dinner table.

The sun had come out, so she skirted the front of the castle and climbed out onto the gray rocks that stood like sentries. From her perch, she turned and took a long look at the unusual structure that had been her home for so many weeks. How much had happened since the day she had first driven her little car to this lonely spot! Would she have come if she had been able to know what the future held?

She thought for a while, and she knew that her decision would have been the same. For many good and positive things had come into her life here. Kent, for one. She felt a warmness creep over her body at the thought of his comforting presence, and she hoped that his still unknown problems would dissolve to leave him able to love her the way that she loved him.

And Scotty. They had built a vibrant and friendly relationship together in her weeks of therapy, and the joy that she had felt in seeing the woman's progress was an accomplishment that she would always carry deeply in her heart. She had learned to care here at Eagle's Watch. She had learned to feel emotion and need and love. And that was worth the danger that had touched her.

She was committed to stay and see this through, to face the threats that surrounded her, to find the motive for it all. But she was scared.

The most obvious motive was the money angle. Someone who felt that her presence in Scotty's world was endangering the hopes that he or she had to inherit. And who could that be? Almost anyone that she had seen so far.

But what if the motive was not such a common one? What if it involved some other aspect of life, a motive that she had not yet considered?

Jealousy? She found that hard to believe. Daisy had shown signs of it in the attention that Mitchell had given her, but Hillary had trouble imagining the blonde, carefree girl calculating the treachery that would have led to the failure of her car brakes. Who else had reason to be jealous? Her mind gave her no answers. It was a puzzle, and she didn't have the solution. Frustrated, and still not relaxed from the day's nerve-wracking happenings, she arose from her perch to climb back down to the house, to the dinner table that she knew would do little to settle her raw nerves.

But then something caught her eye. It was a flash of light, a glimmer, a reflection from the bright summer sun, now quickly receding from the early evening sky. It had come from a movement in the distant turret of the castle. It was the turret that held the many suits of armor that had intrigued her so. Someone was moving the armor up there. And, in moving the gleaming armor had accidentally caught the glare of the sun and reflected it.

Who was in the turret? She scrambled down the remaining rocks with a hammering heart. This was one part of the mysteriousness of Eagle's Watch that she was going to solve immediately. She brushed the dust from her pants and sprinted for the castle door.

Soundlessly, she mounted the stairway two steps at a time. Her adrenaline was flowing. Her pulse was racing. It wasn't until she had traveled down the long hallway toward the rear wing of the castle that her mind slowed enough to think of the consequences of the action she was taking.

Who was in the turret? In a few moments' time, her curiosity would be satisfied, but perhaps she would wish that she had never found out. For if the person who had moved the telltale armor had anything to do with the accidents that had happened to her, who could tell what might happen next?

And suddenly she was aware of the silence in the building around her. Here, far above the kitchen and living areas, far removed from the bedrooms that were occupied by the family members, she was very much alone. Alone except for whoever stealthily occupied the turret she was now nearing. No busy sounds from the house could reach her ears here, and she knew that they would never be able to hear her there. Even if she screamed.

Somewhere in the few seconds that passed as she reached the turret door, the excitement she had felt had turned to fear. She could feel the hair on the back of her neck begin to prickle. She could sense the clamminess of her palms. Was she crazy to have come here alone? Should she turn back and avoid accosting the unknown person who would be lurking on the other side of the thick turret door?

She didn't have time to make her decision. For at that moment the door was thrown open, nearly knocking her slight body against the wall. And a figure stood in the doorway, its masculine silhouette looming large and frighteningly before her.

Though there was a bright light behind him, his features were masked in shadow. He stepped toward her. Her feet were rooted to the spot. She opened her mouth to scream and in horror realized that nothing was coming out. Her vocal chords felt paralyzed. He reached out and took a handful of her hair in his hand. Whether it was his nearness that prodded her to action, or the fear of his touch, she never knew.

But suddenly she found herself tearing down the back hall of the castle, with speed that she had never suspected she possessed. And he was right behind her. She dodged and darted around the corners that she came to, but he never seemed to slow down. She slipped into an alcove that she had never noticed before, out of breath and praying fervently for escape.

She found a small door. It was partially hidden in the wall, a small servants' staircase that led down to the main floor. If only she could make it. The thought of other people below spurred her on. Her feet clamored down the narrow, steep flight.

She turned and looked as she neared the bottom. He was just starting down the flight. She tore on. She reached the lower floor and realized that she had lost her sense of direction in her panic. The kitchen had to be close by! But she was wrong. She barged ahead, coming to a large door that she hoped would lead to voices and rescue. She threw it open and slipped through.

The courtyard! In her panic, she had turned the wrong way and had ended up in the little courtyard that sat in the middle of the castle. Overhead the sky was blue; the high windows of the castle surrounded her on every side. She was trapped. And she was not alone. Her pursuer had arrived.

She heard his panting breath in the doorway behind her and felt doomed. There was no place more to run. She turned to face him.

She gasped. They stared at each other in silence, never moving a muscle.

"Who are you?" he finally asked, his voice a nervous whisper, his brow rolled upward in a frown.

And indeed she had been asking herself the same question. For the man who stood before her, the pursuer who had followed her through the dark castle halls, was a man she had never before laid eyes upon. He was young and dark, with a sulking kind of good looks. He wore a faded pair of jeans and a pale blue work shirt. For all his arduous pursuit, there didn't seem to be a violent bone in his body. Her heart stopped hammering so fearfully.

"I'm Hillary Holt, Miss Scott's nurse. Do you mind telling me why on earth you were chasing me? You scared the life out of me. And who are you?"

"I'm Tony. Tony Raymond. My parents work here at Eagle's Watch."

Mrs. Raymond's son! The one who had run away.

"I thought you were someone else," he said. "And then you ran. I thought you were Angela. That red hair."

She remembered Mitchell telling her of Tony's wife having red hair. He had mistaken Hillary for her.

"So Angela is here at the castle too?" she asked.

"I don't know where Angela is, to tell you the truth. That's why I'm here. Angela left me weeks ago. I've been staying with my parents. When I saw you, I thought she had come back to me."

His face showed the emotional pain that was in his heart, and Hillary felt very sorry for him.

"So it's you who has been polishing the armor?"

"You saw that? Yes, I'm pretty attached to it. I've taken care of it since I was a little kid. Please, Miss Holt, don't tell Miss Scott that I'm here. She'll be so angry. She never did like me."

Hillary watched him quietly. How wrong everyone was about Scotty's personality. How absolutely she had struck fear into them and how startled they would be to know just how much the old woman who owned the castle knew of their goings on. She wouldn't be surprised at all if Scotty wasn't already aware of Tony's return.

They sat on the cracked stone wall that encircled the unused marble fountain in the small courtyard, as the sun went down and cast its soft shadows on the high castle walls. Tony was friendly and talkative, leaning comfortably back and confiding in Hillary in whom he had found a willing listener.

He was a lonely and pensive young man, she found, who had grown up within the gray walls of Eagle's Watch, where his parents had been employed for all of his lifetime. He held a deep love for the surroundings, Hillary could tell, hearing the reverence in his voice as he spoke of the history that had been made through the generations in the Scott family ancestral home. And then a pretty girl, red-haired and very much alive— Angela—had come up to take over some of the household duties, much in the way that Daisy presently worked. She had turned his head and stirred him to action.

His parents and Scotty had deeply disapproved of her, and their impressions had been more accurate than his. But deeply in love, he had burned at their criticism. When Scotty had relieved the girl of her duties, saying that she was undependable and lazy, Tony's anger had flared and he had secretly taken off with her.

Hillary was touched by the emotions that the young man showed as he went on to tell of the pain and disillusionment that had followed. Angela had fulfilled Scotty's and his parents' fears. And then she had run away from him, sure that the world held someone better for her than the son of household servants. He had come home, finally, not knowing where else to go. His parents had kept him, quietly in the servants' wing, worrying about how to announce his return to the mistress of Eagle's Watch, to Miss Scott who had been so angry at his lack of common sense about the girl.

He was still more a boy than a man, Hillary realized suddenly, and she felt very sorry that his love had taken such an unhappy turn.

"I don't think you have to worry about Miss Scott," she said comfortingly. "I think she'll understand!"

"Understand? I'll be lucky of she doesn't turn me out on my ear once she hears I've come back. You don't know how mad she was. She really doesn't like me, that's for sure."

And inwardly Hillary smiled. For Scotty would only concern herself with the welfare of an employee that she truly cared for, a person that she felt had potential. Scotty had wanted to protect him from the girl, certainly. And she would forgive his actions, especially since he gave her a chance to say "I told you so" and to gloat about the fact that she had been right.

"We'll see," she said aloud. "You can't hide forever. And your dad could use some help around here, I'm sure."

"I know. I help him now all I can, always trying to keep out of the line of fire of the family. But maybe, like you say, things'll work out."

He was optimistic, obliging, and Hillary found herself feeling like an older sister to him.

There was no way she could believe that he was involved in the ugly things that had happened at Eagle's Watch. She left him to head for the dining room and the family dinner, glad that she had unraveled a part of the mystery that seemed to hover about the castle. But she was still aware that there were a lot more questions to be answered.

Chapter 15

"Forgive my impertinence," announced Scotty later that evening, "but I seem to notice a subtle difference in the relationship between you and Kent Harris lately. Your womanly wiles finally wearing him down?"

Hillary had to laugh. "That's one way to put it, I guess. I care so much about him, Scotty, but he has things he has to settle first. I'm trying to give him space."

"Smart girl."

"He's so special, Scotty. I'd wait forever for him."

"Good Lord, let's hope not. That would be a tragic loss, and if I may say so, a stupid one."

"Speaking of tragic losses, there's something I want to talk to you about. A true case of disillusioned love."

"Ah." The white head bobbed knowingly, and the eyes lit with their irresistible twinkle. "Young Anthony Raymond. Am I correct?"

"You knew he was back?"

"No. But I'm not surprised. I've been expecting him. Now there's a lad with potential. But he should have listened to me. Instead, he had to take up with that little piece of baggage. Angela, her name was, but anyone less like an angel would be hard to find."

Percival lifted his proud head from the silk pillow that he rested on, majestically yawning, then returned to his comfortable nap.

"She's not with him still, I don't imagine?" Scotty asked.

"No."

"Then he's welcome here, of course, though you understand I'll have to make him squirm a bit. It's in my nature."

"A good dose of 'I told you so'" asked Hillary sarcastically.

"Now don't speak in that self-satisfied tone, Hillary Holt. An old woman must have some enjoyment out of life."

Hillary shook her head in mock disgust, but the corners of her mouth were bowed in a smile. Scotty's spirit never ceased to amuse her.

"Just be easy on him, okay? He's a nice kid."

"All the more reason that he must learn his lesson. But I know he really cared for her. Young love can be so pathetic. Don't worry, I'll be as mild as my reputation allows. By the way, it's good to see you smiling. You've been going round rather long-faced for a young girl who's discovered a romantic future for herself. There must be something else chipping away at you. Care to confide?"

The eyes were clear and direct, and Hillary had to look away. "I—don't know what you mean."

"Well, when the time comes and you want to open up about it," Scotty went on, disregarding Hillary's halfhearted denial, "Just speak up. Now go and fetch that adorable Tony, and let me get this over with."

There was no doubt about it, Hillary firmly told herself as she shut the door behind her and went in search of the hidden boy, one way or another, she was going to have to clear up the shadows that hung over her, before Scotty guessed more than would be healthy for her. She set her jaw and determined to do it.

* * *

"You told her?" Tony's voice revealed the fear that was in his heart as Hillary told him that Scotty was waiting to see him.

Mr. and Mrs. Raymond, faces white and strained, rushed across the kitchen to beat his side.

"You're so cruel. Nurse Holt," wailed Mrs. Raymond, with more show of emotion than Hillary had yet seen her portray. "She'll send my boy away. How could you do this to us?" Pure unhappiness and hurt was etched on the faces of the trio before her.

And why would they react any other way? They, like most people that Scotty had come into contact with in life, saw only the authoritative dictatorial side of the woman for whom they worked. She held the strings to their happiness, their jobs, their homes, the castle that they cared for so much. How could they know that what Hillary had done was for their own good? It was up to her to explain, to ease their pain.

"Please, please, don't be afraid. Miss Scott was bound to find out sooner or later about Tony's return. Don't you see how much angrier she would be at the thought of being deceived?" She turned to Tony. "I told you it would be all right, Tony, and it will. Just go to her."

The tight muscles in his face relaxed. "If you're sure, Hillary, I'll take your word." He turned to his parents. "I'll go to her now, it'll be all right. Nurse Holt wouldn't let us down."

"Wouldn't she?" Mrs. Raymond's mouth was drawn and bitter. "Have you learned nothing in all the trials you've been through, Anthony? I'd hoped you were through with scheming young women. First trusting Angela, now this nurse. She even looks like her."

The small woman was shaking and her husband put a strong, tired arm around her bony shoulders for comfort. "There, there, Mother, it was bound to come out. We'll just have to deal with whatever happens. I trust the nurse myself. Not all young girls are like Angela."

"That's right, Mother." Tony gave her a brief kiss on the cheek and was gone.

"Please don't hate me so, Mrs. Raymond," Hillary said quietly. "Whether you believe it or not, I just want to help."

Mrs. Raymond didn't answer, and with a nod to Hillary, Mr. Raymond led his wife away.

Hillary stood alone in the empty kitchen and hoped fervently that all would go well upstairs.

There was a clatter behind her, and she turned to find that Daisy had entered the kitchen, her arms laden with linen from the dining room.

"Well, if it isn't Nurse Holt," she said with eyes that were less than friendly. "And what are you doing slumming down here in the servants' quarter? I've thought you were a privileged member of the household."

"Daisy, I can't understand why you are so hostile to me." Hillary stood face to face with the young girl, whose wispy blonde hair hung in soft tendrils beside her attractive face. So young and so sweet-looking, and yet her voice was tinged with venom.

"Because it's not fair, that's why. First you come here and get on the good side of Miss Scott, and now I hear the family will be cheated out of their money. Then you go and make eyes at all of the available men around and they spend all their time flitting around you. Mitchell—"

Hillary cut her off. "Daisy, there is not and never will be anything between Mitchell Morrison and myself. I swear that to you. We are just friends. That day that you saw us down on the beach, we were talking about that very fact."

"You saw me?" The blonde girl's eyes shifted away in embarrassment. "I wasn't spying, mind you. I just happened to be walking by..."

She is so young, Hillary thought to herself, so impressionable and emotional.

"I don't care why you were there, Daisy. Like I said, Mitchell and I are just friends, And, if I may add, you above all should know that I have no intention of receiving any of Miss Scott's money, nor does she have any inclination to leave it to me. You were a witness to her will."

The eyes shifted away again. "I didn't see what it said. I didn't look. I just signed my name where the lawyer said to. The page was mostly covered with a sheet of paper. I—I'm not so sneaky as that! I didn't see a thing." She turned on her heel and disappeared from the room, and Hillary felt distinctly uneasy.

Did Daisy in truth know what was in the will? Was there a reason for her nervous behavior just now? But Scotty couldn't have changed her mind about leaving the estate to her relatives. Hillary's forehead was covered with tiny beads of perspiration. She didn't want the money. She had told Scotty that. Scotty couldn't have willed it to her! But even the adamant words didn't ease her mind a bit, for she knew that Priscilla Scott was capable of deciding anything.

Chapter 16

The days went by. The Raymonds' opinion of Hillary changed slowly from hatred to confused respect, as Tony was once again accepted into the household, having faced Scotty's short and intensive lecture on proper behavior. He survived unscathed. His whistle could often be heard around the grounds as he worked alongside his father, easing the daily load and maintaining the property that was a home to him.

To Hillary he was polite and friendly, though it wasn't often that their paths crossed in the course of the day.

Mrs. Raymond even made a few attempts at civility to make up for her harsh words in the kitchen as life returned to an even keel.

Scotty became stronger and stronger. And Hillary's duties were over now, really, but she stayed on with Scotty, feeling pride as the woman continued to progress. The time came when Scotty could move herself around her small world. She had even begun making daily trips up to the tower room where she spent the afternoon hours deeply engrossed in her sculpting. It was frustrating at first, but she gradually became satisfied and proud of her results. She allowed no one to visit her in the studio, with the exception of Percival, who accompanied her on most days, returning downstairs after each session, his black fur dusty with the particles of dry clay that dusted the air.

Hillary gave Scotty the room she needed to be by herself. She asked no questions about the work that she did in the turret, and Scotty offered no comments.

Indeed, their relationship had drifted into an altered one from the closeness that Hillary had first felt when she arrived at Eagle's Watch. They were friendly, yes, and always civil, but the intimacy that they had shared was sadly missing. A barrier had grown between them.

At first, after the lawyer had gone. Hillary had badgered Scotty to convince her to make known the contents of her will, an action the white-haired old woman refused with her lips drawn tightly together. She could see no reason for it, and as Hillary had no way of letting her know of the dangers and accidents, without risking a stressful scene, her hands were tied. So gradually she gave up her attempts to deal with the issue, and merely did her best to stay out of the range of fire of the family's bitter tongues.

Her thoughts of Kent Harris were the bright spots in her days. He had taken over almost all of Dr. Newburg's rounds, as the old physician had become more and more involved with the time-consuming research in his laboratory. And occasionally, in the evening hours when his duties were temporarily done, the young doctor would appear at the door of the castle to see Hillary.

They often sat in the study downstairs, away from the chatter of the family in the living room. Kent seemed exhausted. Hillary felt an ache in her heart each time he arrived, seeing the tenseness in his strong shoulders, the signs of stress on his handsome face. She longed to reach out to him, to hold him close and show the love that enveloped her, but she stifled her yearnings and showed her caring with comforting words instead, sensing that the timing was not right, that the barriers that had been within him from their first meeting still needed to be dealt with.

For there was more than pure tiredness that etched the look of unhappiness on his face, she knew.

There was a conflict going on inside him. And so she contented herself with the knowledge that when the moment arrived for him to take his leave on each of those lovely evenings, he was at least a more relaxed man than he had been on his arrival.

Their conversations were sometimes lively ones. He talked of the world, of some of the patients that he was fond of, of his newly experienced impressions of the northern coast of Maine. Of politics, of so many things.

But when the conversation began to veer toward his future plans, his goals in life, those long dark, shadows that pained her so much would once again become etched on his face. What was he hiding that upset him so much?

She prayed silently on those occasions that the time would come when he would trust her enough to share whatever burden or fear he was carrying deep inside him.

Trust. And did she trust him? He knew about the things that she had faced here at the castle. He often begged her to think of her safety and future and avoid the risk that lurked at Eagle's Watch. And half of her knew that he was right. But still, she couldn't go. She wouldn't go. He didn't press the issue, beyond his constant warnings for her to be careful. And so their relationship began to develop, though sometimes slowly, painfully, with so many words unsaid.

She had never spoken of the circumstances that had brought her to Eagle's Watch, of her feeling of responsibility to Miss Matilda for the many opportunities in her life. She spoke of her love of nursing, of her aspirations to succeed someday as a surgical nurse, of her excitement at the great strides the medical world made daily, and of her pride in being even a small part of such a noble profession.

She longed for each of Kent's visits, for the chance to be close to him, to hear his voice, to watch his handsome face as he spoke to her. And her love grew.

* * *

Summer ended early in northern Maine, and Hillary was surprised to look outside one morning and see the tinges of color that were appearing on some of the trees. Fall was coming. She could not stay at Eagle's Watch forever. She knew that she would have to think about the future, to part with Scotty, to settle things with Kent one way or another. And yet, the puzzles of her accidents were not even close to being solved.

She donned her comfortable clothes, and decided to take a walk by herself, to soak up some of the last rays of the summer sunshine and enjoy the scenery around her.

She moved away from the shoreline, the rhythmic rumble of the waves becoming duller as she walked. She headed down the tree-lined lane that led ultimately to the main road. The fresh air cleared her head and put a smile on her face. She quickened her pace.

Twang! A sharp noise, seeming very close by, made her jump. *Twang!* It rang out again. Her heart leapt into her mouth.

Gunshots! Her feet went into action automatically, and she found herself scrambling over one of the large gray rocks that spotted the woody area. She tried to control her pounding heart.

What on earth was happening? She crouched in silence, her body resting on the soft bed of pine needles behind the rock. Maybe it was a careless hunter, an irresponsible child with a BB gun... a million explanations rose to greet her. But she shoved them all away. She knew it could be no accident. Once again, she was being attacked, scared. Someone was trying to get rid of her.

She felt alone and very frightened. Large tears rolled down her troubled face, but she brushed them away with the sleeve of her shirt. She had to stay calm, she had to stay alert. At first she heard no other sound in the wilderness, and her searching eyes could spot no one. Then the sound of a car engine reached her ears, and she heard a vehicle driving away.

But which way? Under the treetop cover, with the lane turning and curling through the woods, sounds echoed and bounced back and forth, so she had no idea which direction the car had taken. Had it come from town? Was it now sneaking furtively back? Or what?

When the sound had died away, she pulled herself up to her shaking legs and started back for the castle. She couldn't fool herself anymore. Someone—someone she knew—was a raving lunatic. He had to be stopped. She couldn't avoid the issue any longer.

The house was quiet when she returned, as it had been when she left. It was hard to believe that so much had happened since she had walked out the door. But it had happened, and for once she was going to do something about it. For weeks, she had postponed what she realized now was inevitable. These incidents would keep occurring, perhaps even with evil success. The culprit had to be caught. And she would try to cushion Scotty from the psychological blow somehow.

She crossed to the study and dialed Kent's number, desperately needing someone to talk to, needing the reassurance that she knew he would give her.

The phone rang for quite some lime. She was about ready to replace the receiver on the cradle, when it was suddenly answered by a breathless female voice.

The feminine sound startled Hillary, confused her.

"Is Dr. Harris there?" she asked evenly.

"Why no, he's not. This is Pat Hobart. My husband is the keeper of the lighthouse. His phone also rings in our house, and when he's away, we take his calls for him. I'm sorry it took me so long to answer, but I'm alone here, and it takes me a bit of time to maneuver my wheelchair to the phone."

Hillary's pulse returned to normal. At least it was no mysterious female lingering in Kent's home. She remembered that in exchange for the lighthouse quarters he was to aid the keeper's invalid wife.

"This is Hillary Holt, Mrs. Hobart. I'm the nurse at Eagle's Watch."

"Dr. Harris's Hillary? Why, how nice to talk to you. He's spoken of you often."

Hillary's blood ran warm in her veins, and she blushed.

"I'm afraid he's gone away. I don't expect him back until night. Is there a problem with Miss Scott?"

"Well, there's a problem, but Miss Scott's health is more or less fine."

"Dr. Newburg is at home, I believe, if you'd like to get in touch with him."

Hillary rang off with a promise to come and visit the ailing Mrs. Hobart. She dialed Dr. Newburg's number. He would not be as personally comforting as Kent, to be sure, but his advice would be worthwhile, since he was such an old acquaintance of Scotty's.

"Hello." His voice sounded preoccupied, and Hillary had a moment of regret at bothering him.

But when he heard her voice, his became more friendly instantly. "Why, Hillary. How are you? Is Miss Scott all right? Is there some emergency?"

"Oh, no, Doctor, there is no emergency as such, but I needed to confer with someone about something important that needs to be done at Eagle's Watch. When I explain, you'll see why I came to you." And so she related everything that had happened since her arrival at Eagle's Watch—the mirror, the cliff, the car accident, and finally the shots in the woods. He was speechless as he listened to her tale of horror.

"And Dr. Harris knew of this and has done nothing about it?" His voice was indignant.

"Oh, no," Hillary cried in Kent's defense. "He strongly wanted to take measures against it, but I made him promise not to. You see, I've been very worried about what the shock of hearing about this would do to Scotty."

"Quite right, quite right."

"But don't you see, we are going to have to convince her to announce the contents of her will, to show the would-be killer that I've got nothing to do with the inheritance."

"You mean that you aren't named in her will? Then how did this all come about?"

"Well, you see, she enjoys teasing her family. And I'm not sure what she has finally written in her will, but, believe me, I really don't think that she's named me. And we've got to at least bring this all out into the open, and I thought it would be better to have a doctor on hand when she finds it all out. I tried to call Dr. Harris, but he's away for the day."

"Hillary, what you're doing is really very risky, you know. The shock could kill Priscilla. I just don't know."

"But what about me?" Hillary wailed. "The next accident may be more on target, and the shock of that may kill her too. What else can we do?"

"Maybe you should go away, Hillary. Scotty is as strong now as she will ever be. She doesn't need to have a full-time nurse anymore. That will protect both of you, until we can find out who is at the bottom of this."

His words made so much sense, but they were the last that she wanted to hear. She did not want to run away. She did not want to leave Eagle's Watch and Scotty and Kent, with such a shadow over her head.

But she could see no other way. Not right now. There were tears in her eyes as she hung up the phone. She had been too close, too involved to see the picture clearly. She probably should have left long ago. As Kent had suggested. As Dr. Newburg now suggested. She climbed the steps to her room with a heavy heart.

She was standing staring out her window at the huge expanse of blue ocean when Scotty appeared in her doorway.

"The waves sometimes have a way of soothing frayed nerves, don't you think, Hillary?"

She turned to face the clear blue eyes. "I guess so. Scotty, there's something I want to tell you."

"Yes?" The old woman's eyes lit up expectantly, and Hillary bit her lip and said the words that came so hard to her.

"I'm going away now, Scotty. You really don't need me any longer, and I've got to make plans with my own life, you know."

A shadow had come over the white, wrinkled face. "I see. Well, you must do what you think is best."

She turned to leave the room, and Hillary felt as if her heart were breaking. It was all she could do to keep from blurting out the truth, from running to the woman whom she had come to love so.

"Would you tell Mrs. Raymond I'd like a tray in my room this evening, Hillary," she said. "Don't care to join the family for dinner."

I have to go away, Hillary wanted to scream. It's the only way to avoid the eventual tragedy that's bound to come sooner or later to both of us if I stay. Please, please understand, Scotty. But her tongue couldn't say the words. "I'll tell Mrs. Raymond," she said simply.

After Scotty had gone, she considered avoiding the dinner table herself, but decided to face the hostile group, if only to announce her departure.

She took out her few suitcases and began sorting her possessions, wishing that she could get rid of the lump in her throat.

Chapter 17

Dinner was disastrous. There was a heavy feeling in the air, and the comments made by the inhabitants of Eagle's Watch were biting and critical. They picked constantly on each other, easing up only occasionally to join ranks to make snide remarks to Hillary.

At least I don't have to endure this ridiculous behavior any longer, she thought, trying to console herself, but that didn't make her feel much better.

She made her announcement at the end of the meal and braced herself for the barrage that she knew would come.

"Good riddance," Belinda said.

"Having done what you planned to do, you can now take your leave, is that right?" Arnold said.

"Leave the poor girl alone." This was from Mitchell, and she threw him a thankful glance.

"I wouldn't exactly call her a 'poor girl.' Think of what she's going to have in the future," Arnold muttered.

"Found another little rich lady who needs your devoted care?" Belinda snapped.

She bore all that she could, her face muscles taut, and determined not to be goaded into an argument. That was the last thing that she needed at this point. She was very glad when the opportunity came to leave the table.

There was the sound of thunder in the sky as she passed the front door, thunder so loud that she almost didn't hear the knocker outside. She crossed and pulled the massive door open, the wind and beginning rain blowing against her. Would it be Kent? She fervently hoped so.

But it was not. Instead, it was the slight Mr. Browning, the lawyer, looking older and less distinguished as he stood soaking wet in the foyer, the rain running in rivers from his drenched coat.

"I seem to have gotten caught in quite a downpour," he said. "I certainly should have brought along my umbrella, with the sky so threatening, but Miss Scott seemed to think it was imperative that I got here immediately, and I drove off without it."

He removed his wet outer clothing, and Mrs. Raymond appeared from nowhere to take it.

"Miss Scott called you?" Hillary questioned.

"Why, yes, didn't you know? She said she had decided to have a family meeting to disclose her intentions with her estate, and that it was to be tonight."

The relatives had conic from the dining room at his arrival and now stood around him, open-mouthed with surprise.

"My, my, this could be exciting," laughed Mitchell. "Rather like something out of an intriguing novel, wouldn't you say?"

No one answered.

"Well," he went on. "Is anyone going to tell dear Aunt Priscilla of Mr. Browning's arrival, or are we all going to stand here and be consumed by curiosity?"

Hillary spoke up.

"Please, Mr. Browning, I can assure you that none of us knew anything of Miss Scott's plans. She must have made them rather suddenly. Could you perhaps postpone your meeting for a few moments? It's imperative that we have a doctor here, if Miss Scott is going to take part in anything that could be as emotionally unsettling as this meeting could very well be."

"A very good thought, Nurse Holt. If you would care to call the doctor, I'd be delighted to await his arrival before going to Miss Scott. Perhaps a cup of hot tea?" Mrs. Raymond scurried off, and the family ushered him into the living room.

Hillary lifted the receiver and found the telephone line had gone dead, not an unusual occurrence so far out in the country during a storm. Trust the elements to act up at the most inopportune time.

She climbed into the yellow mackintosh that she had worn before, and tied a brightly colored scarf around her head. She would have to drive to get the doctor, and although she didn't relish the trip in such a storm, she was not going to allow Scotty to be submitted to the trauma of this meeting, without medical support. Why on earth had she changed her mind at such a time?

"Well, take your time, Nurse Holt," offered the lawyer, now sitting comfortably, tea in hand, in the living room, where a fire had been lit to warm him up. It's a terrible night outside. "We will wait for your return."

She stumbled along outside in the wind and rain, and made her way to the garage behind the house. She climbed into Scotty's long black car, usually driven by Mr. Raymond, and pulled it carefully out of its parking place. In no time at all she was driving down the road.

She decided to try to find Kent at the lighthouse, as Mrs. Hobart had said he was expected home tonight. It was much closer than Dr. Newburg's home, and she hoped to have Kent's support during the proceedings. She arrived very shortly and parked beneath the bright lighthouse beam, casting its life-saving light far out into the ocean.

She banged on the door of the lighthouse, but her knock went unanswered.

She tied her scarf more tightly around her head, and pushed through the wind to the Hobarts' door. Mr. Hobart opened it almost immediately, dressed from head to toe in his glistening rain gear.

"I'm just on my way out," he explained hurriedly. "I have to get down to town. They're having quite a time at the dock with the storm blowing so violently."

"Come in, come in," called Mrs. Hobart's voice. "You must be Hillary."

Mr. Hobart made his hurried departure, and Hillary entered the cheery house to meet his wife. She looked exactly as Hillary had imagined her after hearing her voice on the phone. Her face was round and creased in smiles, the few wrinkles of middle age only complementing the good-naturedness that was apparent in her features. Her hair was short and dark, and worn very simply, and she propelled her wheelchair across the floor with the ease of one who is very self-sufficient. Hillary admired her on the spot.

"Let me take a look at this girl that Kent has been talking about." She didn't seem to mind a bit that Hillary was standing in her very wet rain gear, dripping on the floor.

"Kent hasn't returned," she explained, when Hillary outlined briefly her need for a doctor. "I guess you'll have to go for Dr. Newburg. It's such a pity about the phone line, but I have to admit it does happen often out here."

She pointed to a nearby chair. "But first, young lady, take off that uncomfortable coat and let me make you a cup of tea. The world won't come to an end if you warm up for a few more moments before facing that brutal weather again." She wheeled into the tiny kitchen and bustled about happily.

Hillary took the wet things off thankfully, and curled up in a big soft chair near the roaring fireplace. She was very wet, despite the raincoat, and the coldness in the air outside had chilled her to the bone. She sat happily before the flames, taking in its wonderful warmth and enjoying the friendly atmosphere of the little house. Here was love and fullness in life. Someday, she hoped to herself, Kent and I may have a place like this. The longing made her heart ache.

Mrs. Hobart returned quickly with a tray across her knees, cups full of steaming tea and homemade crumpets.

"Where did Kent go today?" Hillary asked her.

Pat Hobart frowned for a minute and looked at her pensively and then spoke. "I think I shall be a busybody and tell you, Hillary, though Kent would bop me if he knew. He went into the city to speak to a few people, the most important being a very special doctor who could tell him the verdict that he has been waiting for many months to hear."

"Verdict?" Hillary echoed helplessly.

Pat took a deep breath and went on. "I think I will tell you the whole story. Over a year ago, Kent was a very promising young surgeon at a very prestigious hospital, some distance from here. He was engaged to a young socialite, a girl who meant everything to him at the time, though he's since realized how much deeper his feelings can be." She looked at Hillary meaningfully, and a blush rose in the girl's freckled face.

"Anyway, at the time, he felt quite a lot for this girl. He was popular and talked about and had very high hopes of becoming one of the greatest surgeons in the country. But then one night, on the way home from a party, they came upon an automobile accident along the side of the road. A car had plunged partly over a ragged cliff, and the driver had been instantly killed. However, he had a passenger with him, a young boy who had crawled out of the wreckage and was clinging desperately to the rocky face of the cliff. Gasoline had leaked horribly from the wreck, and there was a great danger of the whole thing going up in an explosion.

"Kent, true to his nature, climbed over the cliff to save the boy, a difficult feat in any circumstances, but even harder in the dark. He reached the child and moved him along the cliff, away from the debris. It exploded. They were safe from the flames, but the vibrations crumbled the part of the ledge that they stood on, and the two fell quite some distance to the ground below. The young lad was uninjured, but Kent..." Her voice broke. "Kent's arm was badly injured, perhaps permanently."

"Oh, my God." The tears were filling Hillary's eyes and running down her checks.

"I'm not telling you this to shock you, Hillary, or to hurt you. I just want you to understand about Kent, about why he acts the way he sometimes does."

"But how could that be? How could I not tell?"

"The damage that was done has healed enough so that it's not easily noticeable. But for Kent, for the skill that he needs in his surgery, it makes all of the difference in the world. You see, all he's ever wanted to be in life was a surgeon, and this ended his dream, at least for a while. Maybe forever. But worst of all, the girl bolted as soon as she heard his career was in jeopardy. She broke up the engagement and stripped him of the emotional support he so badly needed for facing the crisis.

"Believe me." She tapped her wheelchair. "Love can help you face these things. Anyway, his arm slowly healed a bit, and he came up here to work with his father's old associate, hoping to get some perspective in his life, and hoping that time would further heal his arm."

"And the doctor today?"

"He wanted to check Kent's recovery, to see whether the problem was a temporary one, or if the damage is permanent. By now Kent may know whether he will be able to wield a scalpel again."

Hillary's heart was hammering in her chest. "And to think that night he rescued me from the cliff... facing the same situation, risking his arm again." Her voice was choked.

"Because he loves you, Hillary. But he's not been able to tell you, for fear that you would not stay by his side."

"But I would. I would."

Pat smiled. "It is easy for me to see that, but it's hard for a man when he's been through all that he's been through. It seems he found out that you had planned a surgical career yourself, before coming here, and he didn't want to hold you from it."

Hillary rung her hands. "I could kill him for keeping all this to himself. Pat, I would love him and follow him to the end of the earth, no matter what condition he was in."

Pat smiled. "People like you and my husband are few and far between. But there is a great hope that he has recovered, so let us pray that that is his news."

She put her hands on her legs and smiled at Hillary. "You see, I've been stuck in this chair for three long years. After my car accident, at first the doctors thought my case was a hopeless one, and I had accepted that fact. But last year, shortly before his own accident, Kent had been perfecting a new procedure that would make surgery on my own spine now possible. The day may come, Hillary, when I can join my husband for a walk on the shore again."

Hillary crossed over to her and put her arms around her. "Then we both have much to hope for, Pat." Her throat felt very tight.

She remembered the errand she had started off for, forgotten for a short while when she had been engrossed in Pat's story. Now she donned her wet things once more, and prepared to fetch Dr. Newburg.

"Tell Kent to come to me, Pat, as soon as he comes home. No matter what."

Pat smiled understandingly. "You get Dr. Newburg, and I'll send Kent along to Eagle's Watch to join you."

Hillary left her new friend and went forward into the bitterness of the stormy night.
* * *

The doctor's house was ablaze with light, a welcoming sight to Hillary's eyes. She was eager to let him know what was going on at Eagle's Watch, to bring him there with her, and to await for Kent's return. Her mind was alive with thoughts as she slowly understood the deepness of the fears and emotions that had held the man she loved. She would stay by his side, she would love him day after day, forever, no matter what the verdict today would be. She would have to show him, to make him realize that her love for him was far deeper than the love given by his former fiancée.

She parked the car across the street from the doctor's house and hurried to the porch. It seemed like a long time before he answered her knock. He was very surprised to see her standing there.

"Hillary? My goodness, what brings you out on a night like this? You'll catch your death of cold, and we'll have to find a nurse for you, too." She followed him into the house.

"Come back to my lab, Hillary. I was in the middle of something when you arrived. And tell me, what's the problem? You haven't had any more mishaps since I talked to you this afternoon?"

She reassured him that all had been well.

"But I thought over your advice, Doctor."

"Yes?" They had arrived at the laboratory door.

"I decided that you were very right about my presence at Eagle's Watch. Going away was the only solution I could come up with, the only way to save Scotty from becoming upset and remove myself from danger."

"Very smart, young lady," He opened the laboratory door, and the smell of chemicals assailed her nose. The lights were bright here, the whiteness of the walls reflecting the glare. She could see the test tubes and medical equipment on the shiny counters, the books and papers strewn on a big old desk. She had indeed interrupted him in his work.

It was a small laboratory but had the aura of a place where frantic and dedicated work took place.

The doctor resumed his place at one of the gleaming tables, his fingers busied themselves with his equipment as he talked.

"I suppose you'll be leaving then as soon as possible?"

She noticed the perspiration on his brow, standing out profusely despite the cool temperature in the room.

"Well, I was, but then Scotty changed my mind temporarily."

"What!" he exclaimed. "Talked you out of it?"

"No, no, not in so many words. But she changed her own plans, so to speak. She's called the lawyer. That's why I came to get you. She is going to announce her plans tonight. The family's in a tizzy, and I thought you'd better be there."

The doctor's jaw was very tight. His eyes had a peculiar shine to them. "That's very, very unfortunate," he said quietly.

"But, no," she said. "Don't you see? Once she announces to them all that I'm not the one to inherit, the danger will be over. If there is no reason to get me out of the way, then I won't have to go away."

"Hillary, what makes you so sure that she hasn't named you in the will? She's been acting a little strange lately. A little reserved. What if it is you that she's planning to leave it all to? What if it's known, once and for all, that you're to be the heiress of Eagle's Watch?" He was pacing around the room now, wringing his hands. He passed the open door that they had come through and closed it quietly. For some reason, a little knot was beginning to grow in her stomach.

"There's no knowing what Priscilla Scott will say tonight. It could ruin everything." The doctor was walking slowly toward her now, his face very grave, the lines on it standing out harshly in the bright light. His eyes didn't look quite right, and quite impulsively Hillary found herself moving away from him.

"Ruin everything?" she asked quietly. But the truth was beginning to dawn on her. It made her feel very sick inside.

"I'm sorry, Hillary, that I have to do this. But it's a worthwhile sacrifice, you know. You can be proud, in a way."

"Sacrifice?"

He held out the hypodermic needle. "It won't hurt a bit. You'll just go to sleep easily, and then it'll be all over."

She couldn't believe the words she was hearing.

"You!" she cried. "You were responsible for all the things that have happened to me!"

"I'm sorry, Hillary. At first I just wanted you to go away, but now—"

"Why? Oh, why?"

"Because of the money. I have to have some of the money. You see. Priscilla has always promised me that she would leave me a nice chunk of money. Enough that I could give up my practice and have enough to devote the rest of my life to the kind of research that means so much to me. The kind that will mean so much to the world."

"But if she said so, then she will," she said evenly. Change his mind, she thought, say anything! Just let me out of here!

"No, Hillary, since you came, she's been a different woman. She's busy with life again. She loves you. She identifies with you. No, it's easy to see what was happening."

"But I don't want the money. She knows that."

"No matter. And you'd change your tune once you had your hands on it. So you've got to go, young lady, you've got to go before Priscilla dies. Once you're out of the way, she'll return to normal and do what she always planned to do, giving it all to her relatives, as unworthy as they may be, and a nice healthy chunk for me."

"She's reading it tonight. When they find my body, they'll know you did it, and why. You can't get away with it."

He smiled a slow sick smile. "When she hears that you just drove off instead of getting me, left without a trace, she'll be disappointed enough to write a new will. No one will be the wiser, and your friend Kent will be sure that history is repeating itself, that another woman walked out on him. And they'll never find out, they'll never find out."

She was weaving in and out of the tables in the lab now, and he was close behind.

"I'm so sorry, Hillary. You're a great nurse, you know. It will be a loss to the profession. But my research will mean so much more. It's just a question of priorities."

She didn't know whether to sob or to scream. Her head felt light and she had the sense that the room was moving in slow motion. She couldn't make her feet react fast enough. But she mustn't let him catch up with her. Mustn't let him near with the needle. Her hand reached out and tried the door handle as she sped by, but it was locked.

"Help," she cried out, her pulse hammering, her green eyes wide with fear and anguish. This couldn't be happening to her. Not to Hillary Holt.

Dr. Newburg! She should have realized it, realized that his devotion to his work was far too deep to be healthy, that lately he'd hidden even more often behind these lab doors. What a wonderful brain, gone to waste.

And Kent would never know. Her heart lurched as she thought of him. Would she never get the chance to hold him, to either rejoice in his report of total recuperation, or to comfort him and stand by him with her love if the news were bad? Let me out, her mind screamed.

She tripped on an electric cord that crossed the aisle and stumbled into one of the tables. She felt the doctor's warm hand enclose her wrist. I'm younger, she thought wildly. I'm stronger, I can get away. She jerked and pulled herself, but couldn't release herself from his vise-like grip.

She looked into his dark eyes, too close now, and thought. This is it, this is it!

Chapter 18

There was a brief pounding on the door before it burst open and the doorway was filled by a very large frame, a man Hillary couldn't believe she was seeing.

Kent? He bounded across the room with great strides and knocked the hypodermic needle violently from Dr. Newburg's hand. The old man lost his grip on her, and she plummeted to the floor, her heart beginning to beat normally again.

"Hillary!" Kent cried.

"Why?" screamed Dr. Newburg. "Why did she ever have to come here?" Then a terrible cry came from his lips—a cry of agony and Hillary felt a wave of pity for him. His aged body ran through the door.

"Where's he going?" she cried. "He's mad, you know. He'll do something drastic."

"He won't do anything, Hillary. Everything will be all right now."

She vaguely became aware of the sound of sirens in the background.

"The police were right behind me. The house was surrounded. They'll take care of him. He needs a doctor. It's such a pity. Such a waste."

The tears were running freely down her face now, tears of relief, tears of emotion, tears of love. She was all right, she was safe, and Kent was here by her side. She leaned against his broad body and buried her face in his jacket. Outside, the storm still roared, the lightning still flared, but she finally felt safe and warm.

"I don't care," she said before he could talk. "I don't care whether you are a surgeon, or a country doctor, or even a bum. And I'm not going to listen to any more talk about not being able to be involved. You are involved. I love you, Kent Harris, and even if you should decide that you don't want me around, you will have quite a feat ahead of you to get rid of me!"

She looked up at his dark eyes and saw the love pouring from them. "Thank you," he said, and she could tell there was a lump in his throat as large as the one in hers.

"I love you too, Hillary." His hand lifted her chin up and he smiled into her eyes. "But in case you care to know, young lady, my surgical career hasn't been curtailed. The doctor gave me a clean bill of health. My position as a surgeon is waiting for me, and you, my dear," he said, planting a kiss on her forehead, "will be by my side."

They were two happy people as they stood together, in the brightly lit room, a room that had only moments before been a place of horror and panic. Her heart was soaring. She wished the moment could last for all eternity. But the rest of the world had to be faced.

The bustle outside the small house was tremendous. The police cars with their flashing lights and squawking radios were just beginning to disperse through the rain and Kent and Hillary climbed into his car and headed for Eagle's Watch.

"We must be so careful," warned Hillary, a frown creeping onto her brow. "How will we ever explain all this without upsetting Scotty?"

Kent threw back his head and laughed. "Hillary, that was our first mistake in this whole thing. I swear I think Priscilla Scott is stronger than most of us less than half her age. While we've been writhing about, worrying about her weak constitution, she's been seething about being left out of the whole thing!

"It seems she lifted the telephone receiver, Hillary, while you were making your call to Dr. Newburg, today, and heard your whole explanation of everything that has happened. And without batting an eye, I might add. Then she went to your room to give you one more chance to open up to her, and instead you told her you were leaving Eagle's Watch."

"Of course, she knew why, and so she arranged to get the family together with the lawyer, in order to put an end to all the speculation. Your Miss Scott is one of a kind!"

They were pulling up to the front of the castle and were surprised to see a large black limousine parked right before the door. Hand in hand, the two went in.

The house was in an uproar. As they shut the door behind them, shaking the rain off their raincoats, Scotty herself rushed toward them from the living room, throwing her arms around Hillary's neck with a grateful sob.

"Oh, thank goodness you're all right." Then she pulled herself away and looked sternly at Hillary. "Hillary Holt, I swear you must be some kind of a fool to have kept such goings on from me."

Hillary looked at her with a twinkle in her eye. "I hear you just happened to lift the telephone receiver at the right time this afternoon. Where on earth are your manners?"

The bright eyes twinkled back at her, and the white head bobbed with laughter. "Oh, you heard about that, did you? I thought I was so clever calling this meeting tonight. And to think of what nearly happened because of it. I want to hear every word of it, every word. But first"—she took Hillary firmly by the arm, and Hillary was pleased to feel the strength in the long, wrinkled fingers—"I have someone I'd like you to meet."

She guided her into the living room, with Kent close behind. Every member of the family was there, in addition to the Raymonds, Annie the cook, Daisy, and the lawyer. And in the center of the room, a tiny old woman rose to greet her, standing barely five feet high, her dress regal in its high-necked old-fashioned way, her white hair piled high atop her head, much as Scotty's.

No one had to tell Hillary who it was. Her throat closed with emotion.

"Miss Matilda!" she gasped and rushed forward to take the old woman's hands.

The woman's laugh filled the room, a twinkling happy sound as she grasped her great-niece's hands for the first time.

"My Hillary. My dear little Hillary." The two stood and gazed fondly at each other, green eyes studying green eyes, while the rest of the room stood silently around them.

"I must say, my dear, you are the spitting image of your mother, Mary. It does my old heart good to see you standing before me. I've been waiting for this minute for a great many years."

"You have?" Hillary was dumbfounded. "But you never wrote, you never visited."

"I'm a strange old woman, Hillary, as I'm sure you've realized. I was in no position to give you a home, the kind of home a young girl needs, living alone in my eccentric way. I had a rather horrible upbringing by my maidenly aunts, and I had a great fear of doing the same to you. So I lived my life and hoped that you had the character to live yours. I was right. You are Mary's daughter, through and through. I hope you'll forgive me. I must say from all that I've heard, you've turned out rather well."

Hillary smiled at the little woman and squeezed the hands that held hers. She couldn't find the words to express the happiness that she felt in finally getting to know her only living relative.

Hillary and Kent told the story of the incidents that had happened since her arrival at Eagle's Watch, and climaxed their account with the telling of the night's adventures.

"I knew it this afternoon, Hillary, as soon as I overheard quite by accident, my dear—your conversation with him. He's very old, you know, and has always been fanatical about that research. I've been worrying about him lately, not even knowing all of this was going on. But I knew it had to be him. None of the others." Scotty waved a hand around the room. "None of them could have done it. They are either too kind-hearted, or too gutless." She looked slyly at Arnold and Belinda and Herman sitting together on the sofa. Then she gazed at Mitchell, who sat in a chair. "I'll leave you all to your own devices to decide which category you fall into!

"Anyway, you can imagine my horror to hear that you had gone off in search of a doctor, when Kent arrived here without having seen you. I knew you had gone to see Dr. Newburg then, and Kent and I lamented together. I must say, he wasted no time in getting over there."

"I spoke to a psychiatrist at the hospital I was treated at today," said Kent. "A man who had known and worked with Dr. Newburg for years. When he said that it wouldn't surprise him at all if he went off the deep end, I couldn't get here fast enough."

He put an arm around Hillary's shoulders and the two little old women beamed.

"It's about time," Scotty scolded him good-naturedly, shaking a pointed finger at him. "And now, let us do what I called you all together to do."

"But you don't have to now, Scotty," reminded Hillary. "You can do whatever you want to do."

"My dear, I always do just what I want to do. And what I want to do right now is to get this over with." She motioned to Mr. Browning. "The will, please."

He handed her a long white envelope, which she opened carefully. She pulled out a folded piece of paper.

Chapter 19

A deafening silence filled the room, as every occupant sat, eyes glued to Scotty, who stood before them all, immensely enjoying the tension she was creating.

She unfolded the papers and held them up as if to read them, but instead she did a very peculiar thing.

In one hand she held a shiny silver cigarette lighter, and with a mirthful giggle, she flicked the flint and it sprang into flame, igniting the will. She dropped it quickly into a huge nearby ashtray, smiling as the corners curled and burned, the flame enveloping the whole thing until it left nothing but ashes.

No one spoke.

Then Scotty brushed her hands together and looked out at her amazed audience.

"Now," she said, "I have something to say to all of you. All my life I have hated the pettiness and airs that money has given people. And just lately, in this household, I've seen the havoc it can bring even within a family."

Her eyes glared accusingly at her relatives. "I've been aware of the tensions, the rudeness, the suspicions that have surrounded all of us, and finally the greed that led to the ruin of a dear friend of mine." Her eyes glistened with tears at the thought of Dr. Newburg.

"But," she said, "I have finally decided to do something about it."

She cleared her throat. "First of all, I am donating this mausoleum of a place to the state, immediately, to be used as a museum, with the condition," she added with a friendly glance at the Raymond family, who stood, white-faced, in the corner of the room, "that the Raymonds have the right to make their home here, and to work here, for the rest of their lifetimes."

"Miss Scott," the lawyer broke in. "Don't you think it would be better for us to consult a bit about this? You could change your mind -"

"Nonsense!" snapped Priscilla in her authoritative tone. Hillary's lips curled into the trace of a smile. Scotty had made up her mind. No one would ever be able to change it.

Arnold and the Highfields were sputtering on the couch. Scotty addressed them next. "I will settle a satisfactory amount to be put into accounts for each of you." Their gray faces lit up. "But then I will consider my duty to you finished. It will be the last penny that you ever see from me, and I hope I never see you again."

They muttered in surprise amongst themselves, all red in the face.

"And Mitchell," she went on, turning to face him, "there will also be an account set aside for you. It will be adequate to make your adrenaline flow temporarily, I'm sure, but it will be far less than what you'll need to fulfill your dreams. You *do* have the potential to make something of yourself, young man, despite your impish ways. It's up to you from here on out. No more grandiose inheritances to dream about."

Scotty's blue eyes were direct, and Mitchell's twinkled back. "As always. Aunt Priscilla, you've got a knack for calling the shots. You won't hear me complaining."

"Scotty," Hillary broke in. "What are you going to do?"

"I," she announced in a gay voice. "I am running away! I am returning to England with Miss Matilda, where we will share her little townhouse on a pleasant little square in London. I will sculpt all the birds and animals that I please, and get away, at last, from this castle that has been a stone around my neck for so long!"

"Annie." She turned to her faithful cook. "You must come with me. You know I can't abide anyone else's cooking but yours."

The cook gave a hearty laugh, her more than ample bosom heaving as she nodded in agreement. Then Scotty told Daisy she would get a nice check.

Outside, the storm was subsiding. The sky no longer cracked with blazes of lightning. The thunder no longer echoed in their ears. Peace was being restored. The familiar and steady sound of the waves rumbled reassuringly, Kent's hand found Hillary's and he squeezed it happily. "We love each other, and I am in the process of convincing her to marry me," he announced to Scotty and Matilda.

"I should certainly hope so," scolded Scotty. "If anyone was ever meant for each other, it is you two. And I have something for you."

She walked lightly from the room, her head held high, her body moving easily, a healthy tribute to the strength and determination that had driven her to recovery.

When she returned, she held out a large box to Hillary and Kent. They opened it carefully, and lifted out the treasure inside.

"A little wedding present, Hillary, that I hope will remind you of some of the better times we had here at Eagle's Watch."

It was a sculpted eagle, intricately and lovingly formed by Scotty's own hands, its wings majestically spread for flight. Ready, Hillary thought suddenly, like Scotty and herself . Ready to begin another phase of life. Her eyes filled with tears.

How much fuller her life had become since the day she had so grudgingly driven her little car up to the entrance to Eagle's Watch. She had found love, she warmed to the touch of Kent's hands upon her shoulders. She had found fond friendships and self-understanding. It was worth the bad times that had come along with it. For the bad moments had passed, and the future looked bright and happy. The rest of the people in the room began to disperse, all amazed still at Scotty's sudden plans, but all actually satisfied, a tribute to the woman's fairness and sensitivity.

Soon Hillary and Kent stood facing Scotty and Matilda, and Hillary basked in the glow of being with the ones she loved most of all.

"Are you shocked at my decision, Hillary Holt?"

Hillary looked at Scotty with a smile. "I'm proud of you. I couldn't have planned better myself. I hope you don't mind if we come and visit you once in a while."

"You'd just better, if you know what's good for you!"

"Scotty," Hillary said impulsively. "The will you burned—just who were you going to leave the inheritance to?"

Scotty's clear laugh sounded like a ringing bell.

"That, my dear, is my secret!"

The End

Christine Bush lives in scenic Pennsylvania with her family and entertaining cat, Rosie. When she isn't writing, she can be found working as a marriage and family therapist in private practice, or teaching Psychology at a local college as an adjunct professor. Christine loves to hear from readers and writers! You can reach her at:

ChristineABush@aol.com

And learn more about books by Christine Bush at:

www.ChristineBush.com